實踐大學應用外語系講座教授
政治大學英文系兼任教授

陳超明 主編

TOEIC 900! 工作團隊 編寫

全球英語閱讀力

Global English
Reading Power

打造全球英語閱讀力：
觀念及技巧

● 為何閱讀？

台灣的英文閱讀教育多半從國中開始，著重在文字、語言的使用技巧，高中階段側重精讀文章，大學階段則以閱讀文章來吸收專業知識。以上過程顯示，閱讀強調技巧，也就是不斷閱讀，不斷強化語言知識如單字或文法觀念。

但試問學生，為何要閱讀英文，答案大都是要加強英文能力，所謂為閱讀而閱讀，所讀的文章內容為何並不重要，只是要強化文法或增加單字，將閱讀的「手段」當成「目標」！英文閱讀的目標性嚴重不足。

● 到底為何要閱讀英文呢？

從事英文閱讀，其實應該思考以下兩個原則：

① 從目的著手

在閱讀文章之前，先想一想今天我們是為了什麼而閱讀？只是單純想增進英文能力嗎？背後應該還有別的動機，有些人是為了商業、職場而閱讀一些必須的商場或貿易資料；有些為了到國外念書或是閱讀原文教科書來獲取專業知識；亦或是想要閱讀小說，純粹是娛樂消遣；有些是閱讀報章雜誌，吸收新知或瞭解國外情勢。我們閱讀的動機是什麼？值得注意的是，把英文念好是種手段，而非目的。例如，*Time* 雜誌是很多人閱讀的首選，其實只是大家認為英文寫的很好，完全不管自己有無興趣。因此，訂了半年，但往往一期尚未閱讀完，新的一期就已經遞送至家門口，隨著尚未閱讀期刊的累積，想閱讀的意願也逐漸下降。

這種反效果就是因為閱讀的目的性不強。建議讀者要依照自己的喜好來選擇閱讀的文章題材，若是今天我要提升英文能力的主要原因，是商業考量，想以流利的英文撰寫公司文宣，或瞭解華爾街財經走向，那麼就要選擇較具商業性質的文章，才符合閱讀的目的性；如果希望瞭解國外的時尚發展，可以閱讀時尚雜誌；如果閱讀目的不明顯，可以閱讀小說或是軟性的休閒娛樂新聞。

② 閱讀的內容：全球英語或英文經典？

以往使用英文的概念，認為英文只存在課堂間，散見在各種課本或讀本中，強調要閱讀一些經典的作品或優美的文章；但如今英文卻充斥在你我的日常生活中，穿透我們生活中公私領域的界線。讀者閱讀英文應該以資訊的吸收為主要考量，針對需求和興趣，透過英文這項媒介，獲得自己想要的知識和成果，所以在挑選文章時，首重閱讀的內容是否是所需的，而不是為學英文而讀英文。先釐清自己閱讀的目的和閱讀的內容是否配合全球英語的環境，再開始消化英文文章。

以上班族的工作為例，收發客戶信件都是以英文為主要溝通語言，若是英文能力不足，就無法直接瞭解客戶需求進行溝通，獲取先機，喪失市場主導權。下班後，餐廳菜單上出現英文語言，超市食品包裝上也以英文強調重點口味，連外國媒體也會報導異國美食巡禮，若能擁有一定的英文閱讀的水準，這些美食的享用，會更具深度。此外，市場的開放帶來眾多國際品牌的服飾的進駐，許多服裝公司都會另以中文標籤，說明衣物的洗滌方式，但中文標示往往過於簡略或翻譯錯誤，倘若自己能閱讀原文的標示，可能更可以瞭解真正的內容；今日赴國外旅遊時，旅遊書多是以英文介紹當地風光，所購買的物品皆以英文為主要語言，若缺乏英文閱讀能力，將有損旅遊興趣。

當然，我們也可以閱讀經典的英文文章或是充滿經典文學味道的文章或小說。但是，這是一種較進階的閱讀，適合少數想要精進或深入研究英文閱讀的讀者。對於大部份的讀者或英文使用者來說，閱讀全球人士溝通所使用的英文，可能才是現階段最重要的工作。

閱讀全球英語是種起步，也是閱讀英文中重要的過程，它並非最終的目標！

● 閱讀的概念

認識了閱讀的目的與閱讀的內容，我們來談談閱讀的基本理念與技巧。

一般來說，閱讀涵蓋以下三種層次：

一、語意的理解

這是屬於語意學（semantics），包含單字語意、文法、修辭與上下文語意間的理解。我們從小學到高中的英文課程，大抵都偏重語意方面的訓練。

二、文化內容

此部份包含對於支撐語言結構或語意背後的一些文化內涵，例如母語人士的思考方式、教育制度、問問題的方法以及一些社會、經濟、政治制度等，這些都影響閱讀的內容。

三、文章的寫作技巧

英文文章其實依照一些蠻有規則與寫作模式的規範，例如談論事情時，會把細節擺在前面，把論述擺在後面。以本書中談論 Lady Gaga（女神卡卡）的文章為例，文章首段先說明女神卡卡的驚人服裝效果，她穿的生肉洋裝有何特色？造成什麼轟動？再開始解釋她這麼做的目的和效果為何？解釋該服裝如何呼應她的理念。這些都是英文文章或報章雜誌報導的不同寫作手法。

閱讀英文文章，我們可以簡單地從兩個觀念著手，那就是主題句和複合句。好的英文文章一定會有主題句，主題句是一篇文章的菁華所在，點出該文的論述重點。

其次，複合句則是較進階的句子構造，並非只有一個主詞和一個動詞的簡單句，而是以多個主詞、省略主詞、多個動詞、動詞變化（例如：Ving, Ved）等多重結構所組成的長句，常造成讀者的閱讀困難，但若是能搭配本書所介紹的拆句技巧，便能輕鬆解讀長句。

● 閱讀的幾個策略

一、七成單字的原則

閱讀並非得弄懂文章中每一個字，一般來說，只要能看懂文章中的七成的單字即可。面對不懂的單字，千別急著翻開字典查閱，試著檢視上下文和語意，訓練自己猜測該單字的意思。要修正以往非得百分之百看懂文章不可的概念，挑符合自己興趣和英文程度的文章來看，文章中一定會有看不懂的單字，篩選文章時，可以先快速略讀，若發現文章有超過三成以上的單字量是自己看不懂的，或是，十個單字中有三個以上的單字很陌生，有那麼就該換另一篇較簡單的文章，以免減低閱讀興趣和造成事倍功半的效果。

二、挑有興趣的文章

不要強迫自己閱讀沒有興趣的文章，這樣將導致失去閱讀樂趣，閱讀反成了填鴨式教學，挑選文章要有自己的喜好，符合自己的目的性。

三、不要挑有太多文化意涵的文章

太多俚語會增加閱讀困難，除非讀者有專業的需求，才挑選此類文章。

四、要有猜測語意的習慣

別一看到不會的單字就開始查詢，先從上下文語意來猜猜看這單字意思，若該單字重複出現超過三次以上，再開始查閱字典。

● 閱讀技巧

一、增加單字量

英文閱讀的常見字彙量大概在 6000-7000 單字左右，藉著閱讀習慣累積單字量是最便捷的方式，若是一味死背單字，將造成反效果。

二、增加語法的熟悉度

藉著學習本書閱讀技巧，尤其是如何將長句拆解成眾多短詞，有助於加速解析困難語法或是複雜的長句法。

三、知曉文章的重點

要知道文章的重點為何，建議先以短文著手，別一開始就挑選太長的文章。很多人以為，閱讀就是將整篇文章看完，這就是完成閱讀的行為，但是，閱讀應該以抓到文章欲傳達的資訊為主，看完每一段落時，可以先停下來想一想，這一段的重點是什麼？關鍵詞是什麼？與上一段和下一段的重點有什麼關係？作者為什麼如此安排本篇閱讀方式？瞭解文章欲傳達的意思和重點，比看懂英文語言本身還來得重要。

● 閱讀是一種生活習慣

英文閱讀不是一項特別的舉動，也不是特別需要額外挪出時間才能做的行為。相信很多人每天抵達辦公室，第一件事情就是開電腦收取信件，閱讀英文郵件已成必作的工作事項之一。

許多人會瀏覽全球新聞網站以吸收新知，是種不需要特別寫在行事曆上的活動，是出現在每日生中的習慣。若是讀者喜歡閱讀有情節的文章，那麼英文小說將會是最好的選擇之一，可憑自我喜好挑選富有趣味和懸疑性的小說，每天在睡前排出一小時的閱讀時光，享受書海世界的同時，也將閱讀培養成一種生活習慣。（關於此部份，讀者也可以參考筆者所著的《英語即戰力》。）

閱讀英文小說絕對是增強自己閱讀能力最有效的方法，挑選自己有興趣的小說類型，偵探、愛情、懸疑、科幻等不同類型，再看看其中的單字量是否符合前面所說的「七成的原則」。挑選好小說後，開始利用有空的零碎時間閱讀，別正襟危坐地把英文閱讀當成一種課本閱讀或考試閱讀，而應當作一種休閒閱讀而已。

　　個人一直希望國人學習英文，要放眼全球未來的環境，也要考量自身的能力與使用英文的時機，唯有持續的閱讀才能不斷強化自己的英文戰力！

　　《全球英語閱讀力》在《聯合報》支持下，在《聯合報》教育版連載近半年，讀者反應熱烈，促使專欄集結出書，感謝《聯合報》的協助。感謝 TOEIC 900 團隊的李靜儀及政大英文系的博士生呂虹瑾的整理與編寫協助，使本書完整呈現於讀者面前。

實踐大學應用外語系講座教授
政治大學英語系兼任教授

陳超明

如何使用本書

　　本書以全球英語觀點為出發點，主張英文已經與我們生活密不可分，學習英文需建在每日生活的基礎上。（讀者也可以參閱由聯經出版的《全球英語文法》一書）

① 全球英語目標

　　現代生活離不開英文環境，舉凡全球網站、資訊、手冊、工作、旅行等，皆以英文溝通為主要模式，這也是全球人士，母語人士（英、美國家的母語人士）或非母語人士（日、韓、歐洲、阿拉伯人、南美洲人士），所使用的國際溝通語言。

② 全球英語測驗

　　許多像 TOEIC 這種全球英語測驗，都是希望應試者可以將英文融入到生活、學校、職場中，讀者應該在日常生活中培養這部份的閱讀能力，本書的閱讀單元幫助讀者呈現這些考題情境。

本書閱讀單元的重點步驟：

下面以本書討論女神卡卡（Lady Gaga）的文章為例。

① 閱讀重點

並非學習語言技巧，而是藉由內容來達到學習的目的，所以本書先以情境式文章的介紹為主，先瞭解意思，再想文法。

例如：本篇文章是討論女神卡卡（Lady Gaga）的驚人服裝（incredible outfit），和背後的隱藏含意，其閱讀重點是她對自己驚人服裝的解釋、此服裝的保存和處理。

② 文章閱讀

提供「Lady Gaga's Incredible Outfits」文章內文。

③ 學習焦點

例如：本文先說明女神卡卡的驚人服裝效果，再解釋她為什麼這麼做，該服裝的後續保存處理。再一一介紹每段的重點資訊，分析各段落間的連慣性。

④ 語言知識補充站

Vocabulary：每篇文章篩選 5-6 個單字，並提供該單字常見用法，分析它在本文中組成的句子，並教導如何進行拆句，將長句變成短句。

Sentence Pattern：從每篇文章中篩選出一個重點句型，分析何種場合會出現這句型，和閱讀這句型時的強調重心為何。

⑤ 摘要與測驗重點提示

包含閱讀要項、常用字彙句法、測驗重點。

⑥ 練習題

利用閱讀測驗檢釋自己對文章的理解是否正確。文章翻譯與題解列於該篇最後。

⑦ 延伸閱讀及練習題

　　經過以上訓練，再進行一篇類似主題的閱讀練習。

　　依照以上的學習重點，一步一步掌握閱讀的原則與技巧，除了語意的掌握外，對於國際溝通的情境也能熟悉，也就是透過情境的掌握，才能真正瞭解全球英語在國際溝通中的實際運用。

目次

健康環保篇

科普知識篇

職場應用篇

休閒娛樂篇

1

Does Your Dog Watch TV?
狗眼看電視

閱讀重點

本篇文章是討論，狗是否真的能像人類一樣看電視（watch TV），牠們看到的影樣與人類相同嗎？其閱讀重點如下：

① 狗與人類的視覺差異
② 口鼻長短不同的狗所看到影像的差別

文章閱讀

Does your dog watch TV?

Everyone with a dog **claims** his/her pet watches television. However, a dog's view of the world is different from ours, so what does "watching TV" mean for it?

Experts say that dogs will follow movement on screen and may also bark. But a dog doesn't see images <u>the same</u> way <u>as</u> we do. People think that dogs don't see colors; this isn't true. Dogs just don't see as many colors as humans. There are fewer color vision cells in a dog's eye. But dogs have more light and motion **detectors** than we do, so they see better at night. Dogs also see flashing light better than humans. That means they see **individual** pictures in a television sequence, while we see a moving film.

An interesting fact: Dogs with long **muzzles tend** to have extra eye cells for a wide field of vision and motion detection. Dogs with short muzzles tend to be able to see close detail better and are more likely to watch television.

● 學習焦點 ●●

本文先以「狗是否會看電視」來引起讀者的好奇心,接著再比較狗與人的視覺差異狀況。

① 第一段先點出狗主人的看法 "Everyone with a dog claims his / her pet watches television.",認為狗會看電視,其實這句話只對了一半,因為狗看到的世界與人類不同 "...a dog's view of the world is different from ours..."。

② 第二段先破除一般人以為狗是色盲的迷思,"People think that dogs don't see colors...",其實狗只是無法看到跟人類一樣多的顏色 "Dogs just don't see as many colors as humans.",原因是狗的眼球感色細胞較少 "There are fewer color vision cells in a dog's eye."。

③ 接著說明兩者的另一個視覺差異:狗有較多的感光與動作偵測器 "...dogs have more light and motion detectors than we do.",而且對閃爍的光源更敏

1

銳 "Dogs also see flashing light better than humans.";這代表電視對狗來說，是一連串的個別圖片，但是我們看到的則是動態影像 "...they see individual pictures in a television sequence, while we see a moving film."。

④ 第三段談到鼻口長短不同的狗也有視覺的差異：長口鼻的狗可以偵測更寬廣的視野及動作 "...have extra eye cells for a wide field of vision and motion detection."，短口鼻的狗比較能看到眼前的細節，更有可能看電視 "...be able to see close detail better and are more likely to watch television."。

🌐 語言知識補充站 ⋯⋯⋯⋯⋯⋯⋯⋯⋯⋯⋯⋯⋯⋯⋯⋯⋯⋯⋯⋯⋯⋯⋯⋯⋯⋯⋯

★ Vocabulary

＊ claim：【動詞】聲稱
用法：人 + claim + (that) + S + V
Everyone with a dog / claims / his/her pet watches television.
每個養狗的人 / 聲稱 / 自己的寵物會看電視

＊ detector：【名詞】偵測器
Dogs have more light and motion detectors / than we do, / so they see better at night.
狗擁有較多的光線及動作偵測器 / 比人類 / 所以牠們的夜視能力較佳

＊ individual：【修飾語】個別的，個人的
That means / they see individual pictures / in a television sequence, / while we see a moving film.
這代表了 / 牠們看到個別圖片 / 在電視上的連續畫面 / 但我們看到的是動態影像

＊ muzzle：【名詞】指犬科類的鼻口
Dogs with short muzzles / tend to be able to see close detail better / and are more likely to watch television.
短口鼻的狗 / 較能看到眼前的細節 / 更有可能看電視

＊tend：【動詞】傾向，易於

用法：人／事物 + tend to + V

Dogs with long muzzles / tend to have extra eye cells / for a wide field of vision and motion detection.

長口鼻的狗／傾向擁有較多的視覺細胞／以供寬廣視野及動作的偵測

★ Sentence Pattern

句型：S_1 + V_1 + the same as / as（修飾詞）as + S_2 + V_2

S_1 與 S_2 是被比較的兩件事物或人，the same as / as（修飾詞）as 表示兩者在某方面是一樣的；如果以否定方式呈現（V_1 前面有 don't 或 cannot），表示在某方面 S_1 與 S_2 是有差異的。

① A dog doesn't see images the same way as we do.
　　表示狗看影像的方式與我們是不同的。
② Dogs just don't see as many colors as humans.
　　表示狗無法跟人一樣看到那麼多顏色。

摘要與測驗重點提示 ••

★ 閱讀要項

本篇文章須要注意的重點如下：

① 敘述主題：Does your dog watch TV?
② 敘述重點：A dog doesn't see images the same way as we do.
③ 差異原因：fewer color vision cells in a dog's eye; more light and motion detectors; see flashing light better than humans

1

① 聲明某事：人 + claim + (that) + S + V
② 傾向做某事：人 / 事物 + tend to + V
③ 說明兩者在某方面相似：$S_1 + V_1$ + the same as / as（修飾詞）as + $S_2 + V_2$

★ 測驗重點

本文章的重點資訊在說明狗與人類看到的電視影像大不同，鼻口長短不同的狗所看到的影像也不盡相同。

練習題

1. How may a dog respond if he "watches TV" ?

a) Wag his tail.   b) Bark.

c) Lie on the ground.   d) Fall asleep.

2. Why can dogs see better at night than people?

a) Dogs are more sensitive to light.

b) Dogs don't see colors.

c) Dogs have longer muzzles.

d) Dogs always bark at flashing light.

3. Which description is true about a dog's eyesight?

a) Dogs like watching TV more than people.

b) Short-nose dogs are more likely to be TV viewers than long-nose ones.

c) Dogs are colorblind.

d) Dogs have more color vision cells in their eye than other animals.

The Remarkable Purr of a Cat

Cat owners know that cats don't only purr when they are happy, but also when they are scared. Scientists have some news for you.

The frequency of a cat's purr lies between 25 and 150 Hz. This frequency range can stimulate bones to grow or heal. Purring may also release brain chemicals (endorphins) which reduce pain. Experts think purring under pressure is related to endurance. Purring under stress is the cat's mantra, similar to the "Ommm" sound people make when meditating.

A female cat will purr while giving birth. Nobody knows if it's because she's happy to be producing a litter, or because she finds purring to be comforting. Others believe that the purring may speed up the recovery and healing after labor.

A cat's purr ranges from deep rumbles to high-pitched shrills. This depends on the physiology and/or the cat's mood. When cats feel sleepy, they produce a sigh that drops melodically from a high to a low pitch.

Purring has also been known to reduce stress levels in humans and to provide emotional support in times of need. It feels so good when you hold and pet a purring bundle of fur on your lap, and the whole world becomes quiet and peaceful.

Does Your Dog Watch TV？ 狗眼看電視 休閒娛樂篇

1

1. When do cats purr?

a) Anytime

b) When they feel happy

c) When their bones are growing

d) Only when they feel sleepy

2. What are the frequencies of a cat's purr?

a) 26 Hz

b) Between 25 and 100 Hz

c) Between 50 H and 175 Hz

d) 1000 Hz

3. What is the health benefit of owning a cat?

a) It helps release tension.

b) It improves your hearing.

c) It makes your bones grow.

d) It helps you cope with labor pain.

● 文章翻譯 ···

狗眼看電視

　　常聽到養狗的人說他們的狗會看電視。但狗的眼睛所見到的世界和人大不同，所以「看電視」這件事對狗兒們來說到底意味著什麼呢？

　　專家表示狗兒們會隨著電視螢幕上的動作移動，並對著它吠。但是，狗看影像的方式卻與人類不同。人們認為狗是色盲，這其實是錯誤的認知。狗兒只是無法像人類一樣辨識出那麼多色彩。這是因為狗兒眼睛中的視覺色彩細胞較少。但狗身上擁有比人來得靈敏的光線和動作偵測細胞，所以狗的視力在夜晚會比人來得清晰。這表示狗兒在電視的連續鏡頭中看到的是個別的畫面，而人看到的則是動態的影像。

　　一個有趣的事實：長口鼻的狗兒多半擁有特別的視覺細胞，能看到更寬廣的視野和靈敏的動作偵測；短口鼻的狗兒則多半較容易看到眼前的細節，因而會「看電視」的可能性較高。

● 題解 ···

1. 解答：b) 吠叫。

中譯：

如果狗會「看電視」，牠會如何回應？

a) 搖尾巴。　　　　　　　　　　b) 吠叫。

c) 躺在地板上。　　　　　　　　d) 睡著。

題解：根據文章第二段開頭第一句專家的話，可得知狗會對著電視吠，故答案選 b) 最恰當。

2. 解答：a) 狗對光線比較敏感。

中譯：

為什麼狗在夜晚的視力比人類的視力好？

a) 狗對光線比較敏感。

b) 狗無法分辨色彩。

c) 狗有比較長的口鼻。

d) 狗總是對著會閃爍的光線吠叫。

題解：根據文章第二段倒數第二句內文可知，狗因為有較靈敏的光線和動作偵測細胞，因此夜間視力比人來得清晰。

3. 解答：b) 短鼻子的狗比長鼻子的狗更有可能會看電視。

中譯：

下列關於狗的視力的敘述哪一項為真？

a) 狗比人還愛看電視。

b) 短鼻子的狗比長鼻子的狗更有可能會看電視。

c) 狗是色盲。

d) 狗比起其他動物擁有更多色彩視覺細胞。

題解：根據文章最後一段可知，答案 b) 正確。

● 文章翻譯 ‧‧

貓發出的獨特喉音

　　養貓的人都知道貓不只在開心時會出發喉音，害怕時也會。但科學家對此有了新發現。

　　貓發出喉音的頻率大約介於 25 到 150 赫茲 (Hz) 之間，這個頻率的幅度可以促進骨骼生長或癒合。貓發出喉音的同時，會釋放出可減輕疼痛感的大腦胺基酸 (腦內啡)。專家認為受到壓力時發出的喉音與忍耐力有關。壓力下發出的喉音是貓咪在祈禱，類似人在沉思靜坐時發出「嗡……」的聲音。

　　母貓在生產時也會發出喉音。沒有人知道那是因為牠為自己即將產下小貓咪而高興，或是發出喉音可感到舒緩。有人則相信母貓藉由發出喉音，可以加速分娩後的恢復和癒合。

　　貓的喉音從深沉的咕嚕聲到刺耳的尖叫聲都有。這會隨著貓的生理機能和 (或) 心情而定。當貓昏昏欲睡時，牠們會發出一種音調由高而低落下的嘆息聲。

　　這種喉音也有助於人類減低壓力的程度，及在需要時作為情緒的寄託。當你抱著自己養的一團會出聲的小毛球在腿上，感覺很棒，整個世界都會變得寧靜安詳。

1. 解答：b) 當牠們覺得高興時。

中譯：

貓什麼時候會發出喉音？

a) 隨時。　　　　　　　　　　　b) 當牠們覺得高興時。

c) 當牠們的骨骼在發育時。　　　d) 只有在牠們昏昏欲睡的時候。

題解：由文章第一段即可推知，貓在高興時會發出喉音，故答案選 b)。

2. 解答：b) 介於 25 和 100 赫茲之間。

中譯：

貓的喉音頻率為何？

a) 26 赫茲。

b) 介於 25 和 100 赫茲之間。

c) 介於 50 和 175 赫茲之間。

d) 1000 赫茲。

題解：由文章第二段第一句可知，答案選 b)。

3. 解答：a) 可有助於釋放緊張感。

中譯：

養一隻貓可以為健康帶來什麼益處？

a) 可有助於釋放緊張感。

b) 可以增進人的聽力。

c) 會幫助人的骨骼生長。

d) 可以幫助人面對分娩的疼痛感。

題解：由文章最後一段的內容可推知，答案選 a) 最合理。

2

Ghostly Tourist Attraction
靈異之旅的魅力

02

🔆 閱讀重點 ••

本篇文章是介紹一種另類的旅遊行程—倫敦的鬼魂步道（London Ghost Walks），其閱讀重點如下：

① 鬼魂步道的行程內容
② 鬼魂步道的成功原因

🔵 文章閱讀 ••

Ghostly Tourist Attraction

One of the unusual tourist **attractions** in London is the famous "London Ghost Walks," which have been held since 1982. The walks are led by Richard Jones, who has **appeared** on television many times to talk about ghostly activity.

Visitors are taken through East London to the scene of the grisly murders of Jack the Ripper, or to other forgotten parts of the UK's capital in search of phantoms.

One of the things that make these tours so **fascinating** is Richard himself, who is widely known as a world authority on ghosts in the UK and Ireland. He's also a master storyteller and is often given praise by tourists for his **enthusiasm** and dramatic timing.

Due to their popularity, the walks have been copied by other companies, but many have not met with success. It has been **revealed** that some rivals used Richard's books as a guide to organize their own walks!

So if you're in London, <u>why not</u> try a more exciting experience than touring Big Ben or Buckingham Palace?

🌑 學習焦點 ....

本文講述在充滿神祕氣氛的霧都倫敦，來段非比尋常的鬼魂之旅，自然會吸引不少遊客的好奇心。

① 第一段先介紹 "London Ghost Walks" 的緣起，由常上電視談論靈異活動 "ghostly activity" 的 Richard Jones 自 1982 年開始領隊的旅遊行程。

② 第二段解釋這旅遊的行程內容： "...through East London to the scene of the grisly murders of Jack the Ripper, or to other forgotten parts of the UK's capital..." （從倫敦東區開膛手傑克的謀殺現場，到首都內被人遺忘的角落），——尋找鬼魂的蹤跡（in search of phantoms）。

③ 第三段分析該旅程吸引人的原因：Richard 本人是讓該行程如此迷人的原

因之一 "One of the things that make these tours so fascinating is Richard himself.",他是位世界級的鬼魂權威（a world authority on ghosts），也是個說故事高手（a master storyteller）。

④ 第四段點出此行程大受歡迎的效應：許多同業紛紛效尤，但是並不成功，因為他們只會抄襲 Richard 的著作來規劃路線 "...some rivals used Richard's books as a guide to organize their own walks!"。

⑤ 最後建議遊客考慮這類鬼魂步道，給自己一個更刺激的旅遊經驗！

● 語言知識補充站 ···

★ Vocabulary

＊ attraction：【名詞】吸引人的事物

One of the more unusual tourist attractions in London / is the famous "London Ghost Walks," / which have been held / since 1982.
倫敦非比尋常的旅遊景點之一 / 是有名的「倫敦鬼魂步道」/ 已經舉辦 / 自從 1982 年

＊ appear：【動詞】出現；顯露

The walks are led by Richard Jones, / who has appeared on television many times / to talk about ghostly activity.
該行程由 Richard 領隊 / 他曾多次出現在電視上 / 講述有關靈異活動

＊ fascinating：【修飾詞】迷人的；美好的

One of the things / that make these tours so fascinating / is Richard himself, / who is widely known / as a world authority / on ghosts in the UK and Ireland.
其中一件事 / 使這些旅程如此令人著迷 / 是 Richard 本身 / 被廣泛認同 / 當作世界級權威 / 關於英國和愛爾蘭的鬼魂

* enthusiasm：【名詞】熱誠

He is a master storyteller / and is often given praise by tourists / for his enthusiasm / and dramatic timing.

他是位說故事高手 / 常被旅客讚賞 / 由於他的熱誠 / 和戲劇性的時間掌握

* reveal：【動詞】顯示

It has been revealed / that some rivals used Richard's books / as a guide / to organize their own walks!

已經發現 / 有些競爭對手使用 Richard 的書 / 當成是旅遊指南 / 來規劃他們自己的路線

★ **Sentence Pattern**

句型：Why not + V？

此句型常見於口語的對話中，用來向對方提出建議，以在 Why not 後面直接加上原形動詞的方式來呈現。

If you're in London, <u>why not try a more exciting experience</u> than touring Big Ben or Buckingham Palace?

表示向身在倫敦的遊客提出建議：何不嘗試比大笨鍾和白金漢宮更刺激的旅遊經驗？

摘要與測驗重點提示 ••••••••••••••••••••••••••••••••••

★ 閱讀要項

本篇文章須要注意的重點如下：

① 描述對象：London ghost walks led by Richard Jones

② 行程內容：crime scenes and other forgotten parts of the UK's capital

③ 成功因素：Richard makes these tours so fascinating.

★ 常用字彙及句法

在口語中向對方建議的句型：Why not ＋ V？

★ 測驗重點

本文的重點資訊在於 "London Ghost Walks" 的觀光景點及其成功因素。

練習題

1. What place will be included in the "London Ghost Walks" ?

a) Big Ben

b) Buckingham Palace

c) Famous murder sites

d) Modern London landmarks

2. Why did the imitators not succeed?

a) They visited different tourist spots.

b) They only told ghost stories.

c) They didn't interview Richard.

d) They didn't have a great tour guide.

3. Which word would best describe Richard's storytelling?

a) Passive   b) Passionate

c) Aggressive   d) Extreme

The Most Haunted Pub in Cornwall

For many years, the Jamaica Inn in Launceston, Cornwall, has been regarded as one of the most haunted pubs in Britain. When the hosts from the TV show "Most Haunted" came, they said it was the spookiest show they had ever made.

The ghost is said to be a man from the 1800s who was enjoying a drink in this pub. He went outside briefly, having not yet finished his drink. His body was found in the hills the next morning. People have reported hearing footsteps near the bar and think he has come back to finish his drink. In 1911, a man was seen sitting outside the pub who didn't speak to anyone. He was said to closely resemble the dead man.

The Inn was previously used as a hideout for smugglers, and patrons have reported hearing people speaking in an unknown language in the bar. Could this be the language of pirates from the past?

The owners now organize events for people to investigate the ghosts for themselves.

1. What is suggested about the pub?

a) It is situated in Jamaica.

b) It opened for business 50 years ago.

c) The most famous ghost of the pub is said to be a pirate.

d) Smugglers used it in the past.

2. What happened in 1911?

a) A man was killed in the pub.

b) People investigated the ghosts for themselves.

c) A look-alike of the dead man was seen.

d) An event was held in an unknown language.

Ghostly Tourist Attraction 靈異之旅的魅力 休閒娛樂篇

文章閱讀 翻譯與題解

文章翻譯

靈異之旅的魅力

倫敦最稀奇古怪的旅遊景點之一，是從 1982 年即開辦的知名「倫敦鬼魂步道」。這條路線由上過許多次電視，談論靈異活動的理查·瓊斯來導覽。

遊客們被帶領著，穿越倫敦東區到駭人聽聞的開膛手傑克的犯案現場，或是到其他英國市區已經被人遺忘的角落，尋找幽靈的蹤影。

讓這個導覽旅程增色不少的，便是理查本身，他是舉世聞名的英國和愛爾蘭幽靈專家。他也是一位說故事高手，他說故事時流露的熱情，和戲劇性的時程安排，常獲得遊客高度讚賞。

因為他們的知名度，這條路線已經被其他公司模仿，但許多公司都無法如此成功。原來一些競爭對手，只是用理查出版的書，當作指南規劃他們自己的路線！

所以，如果你來到倫敦，何不來試試一趟更刺激的旅程，而非只是去倫敦大笨鐘或白金漢宮一遊。

題解

1. 解答：c) 知名的謀殺案現場

中譯：

下列哪個地方會含蓋在「倫敦鬼魂步道」中？

a) 倫敦大笨鐘

b) 白金漢宮

c）知名的謀殺案現場

d）現代的倫敦地標

題解：本文主要在說明倫敦的靈異之旅，所到地點非一般遊客會去的普通景點，故答案選 c）最適當。

2. **解答**：d）他們沒有很好的導遊解說。

中譯：

為什麼那些模仿者無法成功？

a）他們去參訪不同的旅遊景點。

b）他們只跟遊客說鬼故事。

c）他們沒有去訪問理查。

d）他們沒有很好的導遊解說。

題解：由文章第三和第四段的描述可推知，其他業者之所以無法成功複製這樣的模式，是因為缺乏好的領隊，給予熱情、生動的介紹，故選項 d）最符合。

3. **解答**：b）充滿熱情的

中譯：

下列哪個字最能貼切形容理查說故事的功力？

a）消極被動的

b）充滿熱情的

c）積極挑釁的

d）偏激極端的

題解：由文章第三段的敘述可知，理查能夠熱情且富表演性質地增加說故事時的戲劇性，故答案 b）的形容最貼切。

● 文章翻譯 ....

康沃爾郡裡最鬼影幢幢的俱樂部

康沃爾郡的朗瑟斯頓牙買加小酒館，多年以來已經被視為英國鬧鬼最兇的酒吧。連電視節目「鬼影幢幢」的節目主持人來到這棟屋子時都說：這是他們錄過最令人毛骨悚然的一集。

這裡的幽靈據說是一位 1800 年代經常喜歡來這個俱樂部小酌的客人。他連酒都還沒喝完，只是出去外面一下，卻在隔天早上鄰近的山丘被人發現他的屍體。人們謠傳著在酒吧附近聽到他的腳步聲，可能是他想回來酒吧喝完他那杯酒吧。1911 年，有人看到一位男士坐在俱樂部外面卻不跟任何人交談。據說這位男士跟死去的那位先生長得超像。

這間小酒館先前作為藏匿走私犯的地方，且老主顧曾指出：在吧檯聽到過，有人用聽不懂的語言交談的聲音。這會是聽到來自過去的海盜們使用的語言嗎？

現在的店主舉辦了讓人們自己偵查這些幽靈的系列活動。

1. 解答：d) 走私犯過去曾經利用這個地方。

中譯：

按照文章的描述，這是一間怎樣的小酒館？

a) 它位於牙買加。

b) 它五十年前就開張營業了。

c) 這間酒館最有名的幽靈據說是一位海盜。

d) 走私犯過去曾經利用這個地方。

題解： 由文章第三段可知，這個地方曾用來藏匿走私犯，故答案選 d)。

2. 解答：c) 有人看見一位貌似已經死去的男士。

中譯：

1911 年發生了什麼事情？

a) 一位男士在這間小酒館被殺了。

b) 人們自己來調查這裡的幽靈。

c) 有人看見一位貌似已經死去的男士。

d) 以聽不懂的語言辦了一項活動。

題解： 由第二段末尾的描述可知，答案選 c)。

3

Things Women Do Better than Men
女人我最大

03

閱讀重點

本篇文章討論女性比男性更具優勢的領域，其閱讀重點如下：

① 女性勝出的四個項目
② 優於男性表現的原因

文章閱讀

Things Women Do Better than Men

Drive a Car

According to a study done by Carnegie Mellon University, women are 77% more likely to survive car accidents than men. It's not nagging when you tell your boyfriend to slow down and buckle up!

Interview

A study at the University of Western Ontario found that women handle the stress of a job interview better than men. Women may feel more nervous before an interview, but they **deal with** those fears and practice the interview process with friends and family.

Manage Employees

Many experts believe that women are better in managerial roles, especially in a **service-oriented** economy. They tend to be good listeners and problem solvers, which makes them better at motivating their employees.

Invest Money

A study has shown that women's investment returns **outperform** men's. Although fewer women invest in stocks than men, the ones who do invest in shares are more successful than their male **counterparts**. This may be because women are more cautious, or because they consider the long-term when making decisions.

學習焦點 •••

本文舉出四個一般人印象中男性比較擅長的事情，但是根據實證研究，女性在這些領域上的表現不但不輸男性甚至超越他們。

① 第一項是開車，根據卡內基美隆大學的研究指出，女性比男性多出百分之 77 的車禍存活率 "...women are 77% more likely to survive car accidents than men."。

② 第二項是申請工作的面談：研究顯示，對即將來臨的工作面試，女性比較容

3

易感到緊張，但是她們藉著與朋友或家人演練面試來處理恐懼的情緒（deal with those fears）。

③ 第三是管理員工：許多專家相信女性較擅長管理性職位（better in managerial roles），因為她們是好的聽眾和問題解決者 "They tend to be good listeners and problem solvers..."，也較會激勵員工（motivating their employees）。

④ 第四是有關投資理財：一項研究顯示，雖然女性投資者較少，但成果都不輸男性，這是因為她們較小心謹慎，也以長遠的考慮來做決定 "...they consider the long-term when making decisions."。

🌐 語言知識補充站 ···

★ Vocabulary

＊ according to：根據；依照

用法：according to ＋ 研究報告，S ＋ V

According to a study / done by Carnegie Mellon University, / women are / 77% more likely to survive car accidents / than men.

根據一項研究 / 由 Carnegie Mellon 大學所做的 / 女性高出七成七的比率更可能的 / 在車禍中存活 / 與男性相比。

＊ deal with：應付；處理

用法：人 ＋ deal with ＋ 事情

Women may feel more nervous / before an interview, / but they deal with those fears / and practice the interview process / with friends and family.

女性可能比較感到緊張 / 在面談之前 / 但是她們會處理那些恐懼 / 演練面談過程 / 與朋友及家人

＊ service-oriented：【修飾語】服務導向

Women are better / in managerial roles, / especially in a service-oriented economy.

女性表現更佳 / 在管理的角色上 / 尤其是在服務導向的行業

＊ outperform：【動詞】勝出；超越

A study has shown / that women's investment returns / outperform men's.
一項研究顯示 / 女性投資報酬 / 超越男性的

＊ counterpart：【名詞】對應的人或物

Although fewer women / invest in stocks / than men, / the ones who do invest
in shares / are more successful / than their male counterparts.
雖然較少的女性 / 投資股票 / 與男性相比 / 這些投資股票的女性 / 更為成功 / 與
同樣投資股票的男性相比。

★ Sentence Pattern

句型：Although ＋ S$_1$ ＋ V$_1$, S$_2$ ＋ V$_2$

本句型適用於表達前後資訊出乎意料的反差情況，前半部句子以 Although 所帶
出的子句，表示與後面主要子句有不同情況。

Although fewer women invest in stocks than men, the ones who do invest in
shares are more successful than their male counterparts.

表示投資股票的女性較男性少，但是這些少數的女性投資者，她們的報酬率比
男性投資人更為優秀。

摘要與測驗重點提示 ···

★ 閱讀要項

本篇文章須要注意的重點如下：

① 描述對象：women and men
② 敘述重點：女性勝出男性的四件事情

dive a car, interview, manage employees, invest money

★ 常用字彙及句法

① 根據某研究報告：according to ＋ 研究報告，S ＋ V
② 某人處理某事情：人 ＋ deal with ＋ 事情
③ 表示前後反差的狀況：Although ＋ S_1 ＋ V_1, S_2 ＋ V_2

★ 測驗重點

本文的重點資訊是在哪些方面，女性優於男性的原因。

練習題

1. What is the purpose of this article?

a) To list the similarities between women and men

b) To challenge discrimination against women

c) To illustrate women's advantages over men

d) To emphasize the importance of equality between women and men

2. What can be inferred from this article?

a) Men are less capable of handling stress than women.

b) Men make higher returns on investment than women.

c) Men tend to listen to their employees.

d) Men consider the long term when making financial decisions.

Things You Don't Know about the US Presidents

Dwight D. Eisenhower

The 34th President of the United States, Dwight D. Eisenhower, had a pet dog called Heidi. Heidi was forbidden to enter the White House after she left a smelly pile on the floor of the diplomatic reception room!

John Quincy Adams

John Quincy Adams, the sixth President, used to go for an early morning swim in the Potomac River – completely naked. Can you imagine what would happen if Obama did this today? The media would go crazy.

Abraham Lincoln

Abraham Lincoln, the 16th President of the United States, once owned a general store. When he was 23 years old, he partnered with William Berry and opened a store called Berry and Lincoln. They sold bacon, guns, honey, and liquor.

William Howard Taft

William Howard Taft was the 27th President of the United States. At more than 300 pounds, he was also the fattest President. His great size earned him the nickname "Big Bill." Apparently, he even once got stuck in the White House bathtub. After this

disaster, a larger bathtub was installed to hold four normal-sized men.

Jimmy Carter

The 39th President, Jimmy Carter, was the first US President who claimed to have seen a UFO. He said he saw a large object in the sky about as bright as the moon. It changed color, from white to blue, then to red, then back to white, before disappearing into the distance.

練習題

1. What is the purpose of this article?

a) To tell strange and funny stories of famous people

b) To explore major historical events in the US

c) To list US presidents' achievements

d) To reveal secrets behind some US foreign policies

2. Where would this article most likely appear in a newspaper?

a) Editorial opinions

b) News of current events

c) Classified ads

d) Entertainment section

● 文章翻譯 ......

女人我最大

駕車

根據卡內基美隆大學所作的一項研究顯示,女性較男性在車禍中多了百分之七十七的存活率。所以當女性不斷提醒男友開慢一點,而且要記得繫上安全帶時,絕不是沒道理的碎碎念。

面試

一項加拿大西安大略大學的研究發現,女性在找工作時處理面試壓力的能力優於男性。女性在面試前可能會較男性來得緊張,但她們懂得如何處理恐懼,而且會找朋友和家人協助預演面試的過程。

員工管理

許多專家都相信女性更適合勝任管理者的角色,尤其在服務導向的經濟體。她們會是很好的傾聽者和解決問題的人,而使她們善於激勵員工。

投資理財

一項研究顯示女性投資的報酬率遠優於男性。雖然較少女性從事股票投資,但有投資股票的女性多半比男性來得成功。這可能是因為她們投資時比較小心,或是在作投資決策時較會以長遠的考量來做決定。

1. 解答：c) 展現女性優於男性的地方。

中譯：

本文的主旨為何？

a) 列出女性和男性之間的相似點

b) 反對歧視女性

c) 展現女性優於男性的地方

d) 強調男女平等的重要性

題解：由本文的標題 "Things Women Do Better than Men" 即可推知，文章主要在展現女性優於男性的面向。

2. 解答：a) 面臨壓力時，男性較女性沒有能力處理。

中譯：

由這篇文章可以推知下列哪件事？

a) 面臨壓力時，男性較女性沒有能力處理。

b) 投資時，男性較女性有能力賺取更多報酬。

c) 男性會傾聽他們員工的意見。

d) 男性在做財務決策時會做長期考量。

題解：由文章中列出的第二項「面試」時男女應對的方式可知，男性較沒有能力積極面對壓力，故答案選 a)。

● 文章翻譯 ··

美國總統逸聞趣事

杜威特・艾森豪

美國第三十四任總統杜威特・艾森豪（Dwight D. Eisenhower）養了一隻寵物犬名叫海蒂。自從海蒂留下一坨難聞的排泄物在外交接待室的地板後，就禁止她踏入白宮。

約翰・昆西・亞當斯

美國的第六任總統約翰・昆西・亞當斯（John Quincy Adams）過去習慣一早起床就到波多馬克河晨泳，而且是裸泳。你能想像如果今天的美國總統歐巴馬要是也這麼做的話呢？媒體一定為之瘋狂。

亞伯拉罕・林肯

美國第十六任總統林肯曾擁有一間雜貨店。他二十三歲時和朋友威廉・貝立（William Berry）合夥開了一間名為貝立和林肯（Berry and Lincoln）的店。他們販售的是培根、槍、蜂蜜和酒。

威廉・哈洛德・塔夫特

威廉・哈洛德・塔夫特是美國第二十七任總統。體重超過三百磅的他，也是歷任有史以來最胖的總統。他的超大體型替他贏得「大比爾」（Big Bill）的稱號。他甚至曾經卡在白宮的浴缸裡動彈不得。經過這件事後，白宮因此裝了一個可以容納四個一般人體型的特大浴缸。

吉米・卡特

第三十九任總統卡特是第一位聲稱自己親眼看到幽浮的總統。他說他曾見過一個像月亮那般明亮的巨大物體在天空中。那個物體消失在遠方之前，會不停變換色彩，從白色變藍色，然後轉紅，再從黑色變白色。

 題解

1. 解答：a) 訴說名人的逸聞趣事

中譯：

本文的主旨為何？

a) 訴說名人的逸聞趣事

b) 探索美國重大的歷史事件

c) 列出美國總統的成就

d) 揭露一些美國外交政策背後的祕辛

題解：由本文的內容可知，都在描述美國歷任總統較不為人知的趣聞，故答案選 a)。

2. 解答：d) 休閒娛樂新聞。

中譯：

這篇文章最可能出現在報紙的什麼版面？

a) 社論

b) 時事新聞

c) 分類廣告

d) 休閒娛樂新聞

題解：本文描述的都是名人逸聞，所以最可能出現在休閒娛樂版，故答案選 d)。

4

Amazing Architecture and White Elephants
偉大建物也是蚊子館

🔖 閱讀重點 ••

本篇文章是討論許多曾經主辦過奧運的城市（Olympic host cities）都面臨的問題，其閱讀重點如下：

① 建造奧運場館所引發的質疑
② 後續的維護及使用效率問題

⚫ 文章閱讀 ••

Amazing Architecture and White Elephants

Many are asking what will **happen to** the buildings used for the London Olympics when the Games are over.

The 2012 Games start on 27th July and finish 12th August, and critics have said that <u>due to the massive spending **associated** with the buildings</u>, it will not be cost-effective to hold any activity there, and the buildings will stand empty in the years ahead. Many are claiming these places are "white elephants," or useless and expensive projects.

Many Olympic host cities have faced the same problem. For example, many facilities built when Athens held the Olympics in 2004 haven't recovered their costs. The same problem occurred in Barcelona, host city of the 1992 Summer Olympics.

Another big concern is the cost of maintaining the sites. For example, the swimming pool at The Aquatics Centre will be one of the most expensive in the world to maintain, and there's no guarantee that people will use it in the future.

We all know Londoners love to complain, but here it seems they are complaining with good reason.

學習焦點

四年一度的奧運盛事，在光彩亮麗的外表下，其實潛藏令人憂心的事實：那些專為奧運所蓋的宏偉建築物，在比賽結束後將何去何從？

① 第一段先以質疑的語氣（what will happen to the buildings），點出這些奧運場館未來的命運將是未知數，以引起讀者關注。

② 第二段接著說明，由於這些建物的相關巨大開銷，舉辦任何活動都不划算（"...due to the massive spending associated with the buildings, it will not be cost-effective to hold any activity there"），他們將可能成為所謂的蚊子館（white elephants；指大而無用的東西）。

③ 第三段分析許多奧運主辦城市都面臨相同的問題（"Many Olympic host cities have faced the same problem."），包括雅典及巴塞隆納；高昂的維護

費用，以及賽事之後無法保證會繼續使用它，似乎倫敦人這次抱怨地有道理
（"...it seems they are complaining with good reason."）。

語言知識補充站 ●●

★ Vocabulary

＊ white elephants

指大而無用的東西；在本文裡相當於中文的「蚊子館」。

說明：由於白色大象在古時的泰國視為聖物，要供養一頭白色大象，花費甚鉅，
除了特殊的食物，還得提供場地給絡繹不絕的訪客來朝拜，飼主的財務狀況常
被拖垮，因此被拿來譬喻為「製造財務災難的事物」。

＊ happen to：發生

用法：事情 ＋ happen to ＋ 人／事物

Many are asking / what will happen to the buildings / used for the London
Olympics / when the Games are over.

許多人在問／什麼事會發生在那些建築物上／供倫敦奧運使用的／賽事結束後

＊ associate：【動詞】聯想；相關

用法：人／事物 ＋ be associated with ＋ 人／事物

Due to the massive spending / associated with the buildings, / it will not be
cost-effective / to hold any activity there.

由於鉅額開銷／與建築物相關的／將不符成本效益／在那裡舉辦任何活動

＊ facilities：【名詞】設施

Many facilities / built / when Athens held the Olympics in 2004 / haven't
recovered their costs.

許多設施／被建造的／在 2004 年雅典舉辦奧運時／尚未回收其成本

4

* guarantee：【名詞】保證

The swimming pool / will be one of the most expensive in the world / to maintain, / and there's no guarantee / that people will use it in the future.
游泳池 / 將是世上最貴的之一 / 來維護 / 且不保證 / 人們在未來會使用它

★ Sentence Pattern

句型：due to ＋ 原因, S ＋ V

本句型用來表示由於某個原因，而導致後面的結果（S ＋ V）。

<u>Due to the massive spending associated with the buildings</u>, it will not be cost-effective to hold any activity there.

Due to 後面的 the massive spending 是表示造成後面不敷成本效益的原因。

● 摘要與測驗重點提示 ·····························

★ 閱讀要項

本篇文章須要注意的重點如下：

① 描述對象：the buildings used for the London Olympics
② 敘述重點：what will happen to the buildings when the Games are over
③ 分析原因：the massive spending 巨額花費

★ 常用字彙及句法

① 表示事情發生在人或物身上：事情 ＋ happen to ＋ 人 / 事物

② 說明人或事物相互關聯：人／事物 ＋ be associated with ＋ 人／事物

③ 說明原因：due to ＋ 原因, S ＋ V

★ 測驗重點

本文的重點資訊在於為了奧運所興建的宏偉建築都面臨類似的問題與命運。

練習題

1. What is the tone of this article?

a) Humorous

b) Metaphorical

c) Pessimistic

d) Critical

2. What can we infer about Barcelona?

a) There are many costly facilities that are not being used.

b) There are white elephants in the city zoo.

c) They have already recovered all the costs of hosting the Games.

d) They don't have to maintain the buildings.

3. What does "white elephant" mean in this article?

a) A rare animal

b) An art masterpiece

c) A pricey and impractical construction

d) A collapsed building

休閒娛樂篇

4

Revolutionary New Suit for Horses

An Australian company has created an amazing new suit for horses just in time for London 2012 Olympics, which they've called the Hidez. Looking much like a wetsuit, it has started to attract a lot of attention from professional riders as it works in roughly the same way as the clothing used by runners and cyclists in other events. It has been designed to increase the supply of oxygen to the horse's muscles and reduce muscle soreness and fatigue.

The designer, Mathew Spice, who worked with other elite athletes to develop the suit, claims that Hidez takes only a few minutes to zip on and can be removed very quickly. The material itself is anti-bacterial and has an SPF of 50+, which means the horse will always stay cool. Another bonus is that the horses don't seem to mind wearing it. Although it might look a bit strange, the Hidez suit may be just what is needed to give a horse a competitive edge on the track. It will reach stores worldwide before the Olympic Games begin.

1. What is the purpose of designing the Hidez suit?

a) To avoid sunburns

b) To prevent the rider from getting injured

c) To decrease the horse's muscles pain after exercise

d) To flatter the horse's figure

2. What outfit is the Hidez suit most similar to?

a) Horse riding clothes

b) Aerobics tights

c) Hip hop dancewear

d) Cycling jerseys

3. What can be inferred from the article?

a) People can buy the suit even outside England before the Games start.

b) It will take considerable effort to dress the horses.

c) The suit will affect the scoring system.

d) The suit will start a new fashion trend.

● 文章翻譯 ⋯⋯⋯⋯⋯⋯⋯⋯⋯⋯⋯⋯⋯⋯⋯⋯⋯⋯⋯⋯⋯

偉大的建築也是蚊子館

　　許多人都在問，如果倫敦奧運比賽結束後，那些奧運的建築要用來幹嘛？

　　2012 年的倫敦奧運賽事從 7 月 27 日開幕，到 8 月 12 日結束，許多人已經在批評由於那些建築物的巨大成本，在那舉辦任何活動都不敷成本效益，未來幾年它們將會空蕩蕩地轟立著。許多人稱這些建築為「蚊子館」，或是「貴而無用」之物。

　　許多奧林匹克運動會的主辦城市都面臨著這樣的問題。舉例來說，2004 年雅典舉辦奧運會時，興建的設施至今仍未回收成本。同樣的問題也發生在主辦 1992 年夏季奧運會的城市─巴塞隆納。

　　另外一大顧慮便是場地的維護費用。例如，倫敦奧運水上運動中心的游泳池，將會是全世界場地維護費最昂貴的地方之一，而且還不保證以後人們會去使用。

　　我們都知道倫敦人很愛抱怨，但在這個問題上，看來他們是抱怨有理。

● 題解 ⋯⋯⋯⋯⋯⋯⋯⋯⋯⋯⋯⋯⋯⋯⋯⋯⋯⋯⋯⋯⋯⋯⋯⋯

1. 解答：d) 批判性的

中譯：

本文的語氣是如何？

a) 幽默的

b) 暗喻式的

c) 悲觀的

d) 批判性的

題解：由文章中呈現的觀點和舉例資料可知，本文的性質是具批判性的，故答案選 d) 最貼切。

2. 解答：a) 那裏有許多造價昂貴的設施卻沒被使用。

中譯：我們可以由文章中推論巴塞隆納的狀況是如何呢？

a) 那裡有許多造價昂貴的設施卻沒被使用。

b) 市區的動物園有白色大象。

c) 他們已經完全彌補了主辦比賽的所有成本。

d) 他們不必維護那些建築。

題解：由文章第二段的批判及第三段舉的例子可知，巴塞隆納的情況和其他辦過奧運的城市相似，都面臨建築變成「蚊子館」的問題。

3. 解答：c) 一棟昂貴而不切實際的建築物

中譯：

在本文中 "white elephant" 的意思為何？

a) 一種稀有動物

b) 一件藝術傑作

c) 一棟昂貴而不切實際的建築物

d) 一棟已傾頹的建築

題解：由文章第二段的描述與說明可知，"white elephant" 在這篇文章的意思就是「蚊子館」，故答案選 c)。

文章翻譯

馬兒好風光

　　一間澳洲公司創造出一套專為馬兒設計且令人驚豔的新裝束，剛好趕在 2012 年倫敦奧運會時派上用場，他們稱這套裝束為 Hidez。它看起來比較近似於潛水緊身衣，已經吸引不少專業騎士的注意，它的功能大致上和賽跑選手及自行車騎士等從事其他活動的人穿的裝束作用相仿。該服裝是設計成可增加馬兒肌肉的供氧量，並減少肌肉痠痛和疲勞。

　　和其他運動菁英共同開發出這套裝束的設計師—馬修・史派西（Mathew Spice）聲稱 Hidez 這套衣服只要花幾分鐘就可穿上，也可以快速脫掉。服裝材質本身既抗菌且防曬係數達 50+，意味可以讓馬兒一直保持涼爽。另一個額外的好處是，馬兒似乎不介意穿著它。雖然這套衣服看起來也許有點怪，但 Hidez 卻可以提供馬兒在跑道上所需的競爭利基。在奧運開賽前，這套衣服就會在全球的商店上架。

題解

1. 解答：c) 降低馬兒運動後肌肉疼痛的問題。

中譯：

設計這套 Hidez 裝束的目的為何？

a) 避免曬傷。

b) 防止騎士受傷。

c) 降低馬兒運動後肌肉疼痛的問題。

d) 彰顯馬兒的體態。

題解：由本文第一段末尾可知，這套裝束主要的設計目的是用以減少馬兒肌肉痠痛的狀況。

2. 解答：d) 自行車緊身衣

中譯：

哪一種裝備和 Hidez 裝束最相似？

a) 馬術裝

b) 有氧運動的緊身衣

c) 嘻哈舞者的舞衣

d) 自行車緊身衣

題解：由文章第一段內容描述可推知，自行車裝束和這套衣服最相近，故答案選 d)。

3. 解答：a) 奧運開賽前人們還可以在英國以外的地方買到這套裝束。

中譯：

中譯：由這篇文章可以推論得知下面哪個選項？

a) 奧運開賽前人們還可以在英國以外的地方買到這套裝束。

b) 要花相當大的力氣，才能幫馬兒穿上這套衣服。

c) 這套衣服會影響比賽計分系統。

d) 這套衣服會引領一波嶄新的流行趨勢。

題解：由文章末尾最後一句話可知，選項 a) 正確。

焦點特寫篇

5

The Royal Wedding
皇室婚禮

閱讀重點

英文閱讀除了單字與句法的熟悉外,最重要是掌握資訊重點,以提升快速閱讀的能力,本文以 2011 年英國皇室婚禮(British royal wedding)為主題,其閱讀重點如下:

① 本文屬於新聞報導,為吸引讀者,會將最引人注目的內容放在第一段:英國皇室婚禮的新娘禮服終於亮相了。

② 全文強調設計者的設計感想:
畢生難忘的經驗(the experience of a lifetime),才是本文資訊所在。

文章閱讀

The Royal Wedding

The wait is over. Prince William and Catherine Middleton are married, and fashion lovers around the world have finally seen it: the royal wedding gown. The dress had been the subject of much

speculation ever since the royal couple got engaged.

The wedding dress was **designed** by Sarah Burton, who kept the project a secret. Not even her best friends knew that she was designing the royal wedding dress.

"It has been the experience of a lifetime to work with Catherine Middleton to create her wedding dress, and I have enjoyed every moment of it," said Burton. "Catherine looked absolutely **stunning**, and I am **delighted** that the dress represents the best of British craftsmanship."

學習焦點 ···

本文簡要敘述 2011 年 4 月英國威廉王子（Prince William）與 Kate Middleton 的世紀婚禮中最熱門的話題 — 新娘禮服。

① 第一句以 "The wait is over." 引起讀者的好奇，不同於一般文章的話說從頭，本文從讀者立場出發，說「等待已經結束了」。大家等待的是一睹新娘禮服的時刻，接下去引出主題："…fashion lovers around the world have finally seen it: the royal wedding gown."

② 第二段承接第一段的新娘禮服話題，帶出禮服的設計師："The wedding dress was designed by Sarah Burton…"；"Not even her best friends knew that she was designing the royal wedding dress."（同時她為了保密，連她最好的朋友都不知道她在設計禮服）。

③ 第三段敘述 Sarah Burton 很享受工作過程中的每一刻時光 "I have enjoyed

5

every moment of it,..." ，也對禮服能表現出英國最佳的手藝技巧感到欣慰 "I am delighted that the dress represents the best of British craftsmanship." 。

🔵 語言知識補充站 ⋯⋯⋯⋯⋯⋯⋯⋯⋯⋯⋯⋯⋯⋯⋯⋯⋯⋯⋯⋯⋯

★ **Vocabulary**

＊ royal：【修飾語】王室的

用法：royal ＋ 名詞

Fashion lovers / around the world / have finally seen it: / the royal wedding gown.

時尚愛好者 / 全世界 / 終於看到它 / 皇室新娘禮服

＊ speculation：【名詞】推測

The dress / had been the subject of / much speculation / ever since the royal couple got engaged.

這件衣服 / 已成為話題 / 許多推測 / 自從皇室夫婦訂婚以來

＊ design：【動詞】設計

用法：人 ＋ design ＋ 事物；事物 ＋ be designed by ＋ 人

The wedding dress / was designed by / Sarah Burton, / who kept the project a secret.

這件結婚禮服 / 由⋯⋯設計 / 莎拉波頓 / 她視此專案為機密

＊ stunning：【修飾語】令人震驚的；驚為天人的

用法：人 ＋ look(s) ＋ stunning；stunning ＋ 名詞

Catherine / looked / absolutely stunning.

凱薩琳 / 看起來 / 絕對是驚為天人的

＊ delight：【動詞】高興；欣喜

用法：人 ＋ be delighted ＋ that ＋ S ＋ V

I am delighted that / the dress / represents the best of / British craftsmanship.

我感到高興 / 這件衣服 / 代表最佳的 / 英國手藝技巧

★ Sentence Pattern

句型："...," says / said ＋ 人 或 人 ＋ says / said "... ."

此種句型稱為引述句，目的是藉著引述的句子，還原當事人說過的話，呈現較為客觀或真實的角度，常用於報導性的文章，如新聞內容。

"It has been the experience of a lifetime to work with Catherine Middleton to create her wedding dress, and I have enjoyed every moment of it," said Burton.

代表設計師 Sarah Burton 當時說的話

引號中的句子代表 Burton 自己對於設計禮服的看法：與 Catherine Middleton 工作是畢生難忘的經驗，我享受過程中的每一刻時光。

摘要與測驗重點提示 ●●●●●●●●●●●●●●●●●●●●●●●●●●●●●

★ 閱讀要項

新聞報導通常是將最引人注意的放在第一段，其後文章呈倒三角形，也就是重要的放前面，其餘細節放後面。新聞文章通常包括 5W ＋ 1H：

- who：Prince William, Catherine Middleton and fashion lovers
- what：royal wedding gown
- when：when they are married

- where：around the world
- why：The dress had been the subject of much speculation ever since the royal couple got engaged.

新聞報導較常見的句法是引述句：

"...," + says / said + 人。希望引用人物自己的話語以較為客觀的角度呈現。

本文的重點是大家最關注的英國皇室婚禮話題：新娘禮服、服設計者以及設計師個人感想。

練習題

1. According to the article, what is the most anticipated thing for fashion lovers?

a) The bride's age

b) The bridegroom's outfit

c) The bride's dress

d) The wedding reception decoration

2. What is suggested about Sarah Burton in this article?

a) She thought the project was extremely difficult.

b) She was not satisfied with her work.

c) She didn't get along with the bride.

d) She was undertaking a top secret project.

Adidas Expecting a Boost in India

Adidas, the German sportswear manufacturer, has announced it will start selling its sports shoes in India. Each pair will cost only one dollar.

"The shoes will be sold in villages through a distribution network," Adidas CEO Herbert Hainer said. Adidas has revealed that its other company Reebok will be responsible for the manufacturing and marketing side of the campaign. India is expected to become the world's most populated country in the next few years.

Can Adidas persuade people in villages across India to trade their plastic sandals for a pair of inexpensive sneakers made by a global brand? If yes, the doors will open to a huge new market. In the rest of the world, people are wondering why they have to pay $100 for a pair of Adidas shoes.

1. Why does Adidas plan to sell shoes in India?

a) India is a rich country.

b) The company has already built a solid customer base there.

c) India is a potential market for sneakers.

d) Indian people like to wear sneakers.

2. What can be inferred from the passages?

a) Adidas will sell sneakers in India at an affordable price.

b) Adidas sells sneakers at the same price around the world.

c) Adidas competes seriously with Reebok in the Indian market.

d) They will only sell sneakers to the wealthiest people in India.

3. How will Adidas sell sports shoes in India?

a) Through door-to-door sales

b) Through a marketing network

c) Through the local government

d) Through word of mouth

文章閱讀 翻譯與題解

文章翻譯

皇室婚禮

等待終於結束了。威廉王子與凱薩琳・密道頓已經完婚，而全球的時尚愛好者們終於見識到皇室婚禮的婚紗。這對皇室佳偶的禮服在他們訂婚之初，就成為眾所期待的焦點。

這套婚紗禮服由莎拉・伯頓所設計。她對此任務保密到家，就連她最要好的朋友也不知道她正在為皇室的婚禮設計婚紗。

「為凱薩琳・密道頓設計婚紗禮服是畢生難忘的經驗，工作的過程裡，我每分每秒都樂在其中。」她提到：「凱薩琳看來真的美極了，而我很高興這套婚紗充分展現了英國極致的手工藝。」

題解

1. 解答：c) 新娘的婚紗

中譯：

根據這篇短文，令時尚愛好者們最引頸企盼的事情為何？

a) 新娘的年齡

b) 新郎的服裝

c) 新娘的婚紗

d) 婚宴的佈置

題解：由文章第一段中的 fashion lovers（時尚愛好者）、the dress（禮服）、the subject of much speculation（眾所期待的焦點）等關鍵字詞可知，時尚人士期待知道新娘會穿著怎樣的婚紗。故答案選 c)。

2. 解答：d）她正進行一項高度機密的任務。

中譯：

關於 Sarah Burton，文章中提到了什麼？

a）她認為這個任務非常困難。

b）她不滿意她自己的作品。

c）她與新娘相處不睦。

d）她正進行一項高度機密的任務。

題解：由文章第二段提到 keep a secret（保密）、not even her best friends knew（連她最要好的朋友也不知道），可見這是極為機密（top-secret）的任務，故答案選 d）最恰當。

● 文章翻譯 ....

愛迪達期望在印度有高成長

德國休閒運動用品製造商愛迪達宣佈將開始在印度銷售該品牌的運動鞋。一雙鞋只需要價一美金。

該公司執行長 Herbert Hainer 說：「運動鞋會透過經銷網絡在鄉村販售」。愛迪達已經透露它的分公司銳跑將會負責生產製造及行銷活動。預期印度在未來幾年將會成為全球人口最多的國家。

愛迪達是否能說服印度鄉間的居民將他們的塑膠涼鞋換成一家全球品牌所製造的平價球鞋呢？如果可以，一個龐大的新興市場大門即將敞開。但在世界其他地區的人們會不禁懷疑，為什麼他們要花一百美金買一雙愛迪達球鞋。

● 題解 ....

1. 解答：c) 因為對球鞋而言，印度是個很有潛力的市場。

中譯：

為什麼愛迪達計畫在印度販售球鞋？

a) 因為印度是個富裕國家。

b) 因為該公司已經在印度建立了忠實客群。

c) 因為對球鞋而言，印度是個很有潛力的市場。

d) 因為印度人喜歡穿球鞋。

題解：由文章後半段的關鍵句 "India is expected to become the world's most populated country in the next few years." 可知，全國人口眾多的印度是個極有潛力的新興市場（new market），故答案選 c) 最適合。

2. 解答：a) 愛迪達將在印度販售價格低廉的球鞋。

中譯：

由這段短文可得知什麼？

a) 愛迪達將在印度販售價格低廉的球鞋。

b) 愛迪達的球鞋將在全球以統一的價格銷售。

c) 愛迪達和銳跑彼此在印度市場競爭激烈。

d) 它們只將球鞋賣給印度最有錢的一群人。

題解：由文章中的關鍵句 "Each pair will cost only one dollar." 和 "The shoes will be sold in villages..." 可知，愛迪達計畫將球鞋賣到鄉村，而且主打人人買得起的低廉價格，深入印度鄉間，故答案為 a)。

3. 解答：b) 透過行銷網路

中譯：

愛迪達打算如何在印度銷售球鞋？

a) 採取登門造訪的銷售法

b) 透過行銷網路

c) 透過地方政府

d) 透過口耳相傳

題解：How 問的是行銷「方式、管道」，從文章關鍵句 "The shoe will be sold...through a distribution network."，得知是透過「行銷網路」的銷售方式，答案為 b) 最適當。distribution 是指「經銷」，network 則是「網路；網絡」。

The Delivery Guy Who Saw
Jeremy Lin Coming
預見「林來瘋」

(06)

閱讀重點

本篇文章是敘述一名快遞員 Ed Weiland 因為曾在網站上預測 Jeremy Lin 有機會成為 NBA 明日之星，在 "Linsanity" 成為風潮後，他也因此成為眾人追尋的對象，其閱讀重點如下：

① ED Weiland 的預測
② Jeremy Lin 的崛起與其對 Ed Weiland 的影響

文章閱讀

The Delivery Guy Who Saw Jeremy Lin Coming

In May 2010, a FedEx driver named Ed Weiland wrote about basketball player Jeremy Lin for the Hoops Analyst website. Back then, Lin was an **unknown** point guard who had completed his final season at Harvard. Weiland noted that Lin's performances **compared favorably with** those of NBA guards like Allen Iverson and Gary Payton. Weiland wrote: "Jeremy Lin will be good enough to start in the NBA and possibly star."

After Lin's rise, Weiland's post was **circulated** on the Internet. Web users **crashed** the Hoops Analyst website after Lin's team beat the Lakers by 38 points. Ed Weiland's analysis has been compared to the method of predicting success in Major League Baseball portrayed in *"Moneyball"*, an Oscar nominated baseball film starring Brad Pitt.

Weiland was amused by the **appreciation** of his work, but in fact, he never expected Lin to create such "Linsanity."

學習焦點 ••

快遞員 Ed Weiland 早在林書豪成名前，就能夠慧眼識英雄，在網站上預測林的潛力，本文藉此事件來凸顯「林來瘋」的熱潮現象。

① 第一段先指出 2010 年有一位快遞員 Ed Weiland 在 Hoops Analyst 網站上，發表他對當時沒沒無聞的林書豪的看法，認為林的表現可媲美 NBA 當紅球星 "Lin's performances compared favorably with those of NBA guards like Allen Iverson and Gary Payton."，並預測林會成為明日之星 "Jeremy Lin will be good enough to start in the NBA and possibly star."。

② 第二段敘述林書豪一戰成名後，Weiland 之前在網站上的發文被廣為流傳 "After Lin's rise, Weiland's post was circulated on the Internet."，而他所做的分析也被拿來與電影「魔球」中預測大聯盟勝率的方法相較，"Ed Weiland's analysis has been compared to the method of predicting success in Major League Baseball portrayed in Moneyball."。

③ 第三段以 Weiland 自己從來沒有預期林書豪會創造出如此大的旋風做結語：
　"...he never expected Lin to create such 'Linsanity.' "。

● 語言知識補充站 ●●●●●●●●●●●●●●●●●●●●●●●●●●●●●●●●●●●●●

★ Vocabulary

＊ unknown：【修飾語】不知名的

Back then, / Lin was an unknown point guard / who had completed his final season at Harvard.

那時 / Jeremy Lin 是一位沒沒無聞的控球後衛 / 才結束他在哈佛大學的最後一季賽事

＊ compare favorably with：媲美；匹敵

用法：人₁ / 事物₁ ＋ compare favorably with ＋ 人₂ / 事物₂

Weiland noted / that Lin's performances / compared favorably with / those of NBA guards.

Weiland 注意到 / Lin 的表現 / 可媲美 / 一些 NBA 後衛的表現

＊ circulate：【動詞】使傳播；使流通

用法：文章 / 訊息 ＋ be circulated ＋ 流通地點

Weiland's post / was circulated / on the Internet.

Weiland 的貼文 / 被流傳 / 在網路上

＊ crash：【動詞】（電腦設備）當機

Web users / crashed the Hoops Analyst website / after Lin's team beat the Lakers / by 38 points.

網友 / 癱瘓了 Hoops Analyst 網站 / 在 Lin 的球隊擊敗湖人隊後 / 以 38 分

＊ appreciation：【名詞】賞識；感激。

Weiland was amused / by the appreciation of his work /, but in fact, / he never expected / Lin to create such "Linsanity."

Weiland 感到高興 / 因他的文章得到的賞識 / 但事實上 / 他從未預期 / Lin 會創造出如此大的旋風

★ Sentence Pattern

句型：S_1 + V_1 + after + S_2 + V_2

After 後面帶出來的句子是表示一個時間點，意即 V_1 是在 V_2 發生之後才出現的動作。

Web users crashed the Hoops Analyst website <u>after Lin's team beat the Lakers by 38 points.</u>

表示林書豪打敗（V_2）湖人隊之後，網友癱瘓（V_1）了 Hoops Analyst 網站

摘要與測驗重點提示 ●●●●●●●●●●●●●●●●●●●●●●●●●●●●●●●●●

★ 閱讀要項

本篇文章須要注意的重點如下：

① 敘述主題：Ed Weiland saw Jeremy Lin coming.
② 敘述重點：Weiland predicted that Lin would be good enough to start in the NBA and possibly star.
③ 後續影響：Web users crashed the Hoops Analyst website.

① 訊息流通：文章 / 訊息 ＋ be circulated ＋ 流通地點
② 相互匹敵：人₁ / 事物₁ ＋ compare favorably with ＋ 人₂ / 事物₂

★ 測驗重點

本文章的重點資訊在於 Weiland 對 Lin 的預測，並預測成功後對 Weiland 的影響。

練習題

1. Who is Ed Weiland?

a) An NBA star
b) A professional sports analyst
c) A delivery man
d) An actor

2. Why was there an instant surge of traffic to the Hoops Analyst website?

a) Because Jeremy completed his final season at Harvard

b) Because people searched for Weiland's post

c) Because Jeremy posted a comment on the site

d) Because there was a report about Weiland's story

3. What did Weiland say in his post?

a) He described the rise of "Linsanity."

b) He predicted that Lin would become a star.

c) He announced that Gary Payton would be the next NBA star.

d) He made a comparison between Lin and Brad Pitt.

延伸閱讀 •••

Lessons Learned from "Linsanity"

You may not be a basketball star, but Jeremy Lin's story offers important lessons for planning your career.

1. Set Goals

Firstly, career success means having a goal. Jeremy has been clear about this. He stayed focused on his goal despite many challenges and rejections.

2. Humility

Lin is commended for his humility. He has excelled by accepting advice from people with experience and knows that others are attracted to confidence, not arrogance.

3. Perseverance

His Harvard degree positioned Lin well for a successful career outside of basketball. When Lin was rejected by teams before the Knicks swooped, he could have given up and chosen another path. Instead, he persevered, and it has paid off enormously.

4. Find Ways to Add Value

You have to show people what you can do for them, and earn the attention of your peers and those above you.

5. Versatility

The difference between Lin and other players is that he always has a backup plan. If the Knicks hadn't recognized his potential, his education would be serving him just as well.

練習題

1. Why are people attracted to Lin's humility?

a) They like listening to people.

b) They like arrogant people.

c) They like his experience.

d) They like confident people.

2. According to the article, why is Lin different from other players?

a) He set his life goals when he was a child.

b) He is commended for being hardworking.

c) He possesses an excellent academic background.

d) He has become an asset for his team.

3. In the context of the article, what does "peers" mean?

a) Your boss

b) Your co-workers

c) Your family

d) Your friends

文章翻譯

預見「林來瘋」

　　2010 年五月，一位聯邦快遞的司機名叫艾德・威蘭（Ed Weiland）在〈籃圈分析網〉寫了關於籃球選手林書豪的評論。回到當時，林書豪只是一名剛打完哈佛季末賽，沒沒無聞的控球後衛。威蘭卻注意到林書豪的表現可媲美一些 NBA 後衛選手像是艾倫・艾佛森（Allen Iverson）和蓋瑞・珮頓（Gary Payton）。威蘭寫道：「林書豪將會好到得以進入 NBA，且可能成為籃球界的明星。」

　　林書豪真的崛起之後，威蘭的評論文章在網路不斷流傳。林書豪的球隊以多出 38 分的佳績，擊敗湖人隊後，網路客更癱瘓了該網站。艾德・威蘭的分析被比擬為電影《魔球》中所描繪預測棒球大聯盟勝率的方式，該電影獲奧斯卡提名，並由布萊德・彼特（Brad Pitt）擔綱演出。

　　威蘭因為他的分析受讚賞而高興，但事實上，他從沒料到林書豪會創造出「林來瘋」這樣的現象。

題解

1. 解答：c）一位送貨員

中譯：

誰是艾德・威蘭（Ed Weiland）？

a）一位 NBA 明星

b）一位專業的運動競賽分析師

c) 一位送貨員

d) 一個男演員

題解：由文章第一段的描述可知，艾德‧威蘭是一位送貨員。

2. 解答：b) 因為人們上網搜尋威蘭發表在該網站的文章。

中譯：

為什麼籃圈分析網會瞬間被網民蜂擁觀看？

a) 因為林書豪打完了他在哈佛的季末賽。

b) 因為人們上網搜尋威蘭發表在該網站的文章。

c) 因為林書豪在該網站發表了一篇評論。

d) 因為網站上有一篇關於威蘭故事的報導。

題解：由文章第二段內容可推知，因為大家都想去看威蘭發表的分析文章，所以塞爆了該網站。

3. 解答：b) 他預測林書豪將會成為明日之星。

中譯：

威蘭在他所發表的文章中分析了什麼？

a) 他描述了「林來瘋」的崛起。

b) 他預測林書豪將會成為明日之星。

c) 他宣布蓋瑞‧珮頓會成為下屆 NBA 球星。

d) 他比較了林書豪和布萊德‧彼特。

題解：由文章第二段末尾可知，威蘭的文章之所以廣為人知，是因為他預測出林書豪可能成為明日之星。

● 文章翻譯 ···

「林來瘋」的啟示

你也許不會成為一位籃球明星，但林書豪的故事可以為人們的未來生涯規劃提供重要的一課。

1. 設定目標

首先，成功的生涯規劃意味著要有目標。林書豪一直很清楚這點。儘管面臨許多挑戰和拒絕，仍持續專注於他的目標。

2. 謙虛

林書豪的謙遜態度廣受讚揚。他能勝出的特點，在於能夠接受有經驗者的忠告，且深知人們是被自信所吸引，而非自大。

3. 堅持不懈

他的哈佛學歷可以為他在籃球界之外的領域帶來成功的生涯。在他被其他球隊拒絕，進入紐約尼克隊之前，他大可就此放棄轉而選擇另一條路發展。但他堅持不懈，獲致巨大的成功。

4. 找方法為自己加值

你必須讓人們知道你能為他們做什麼，進而獲得同儕及上司的注意。

5. 多才多藝

林書豪與其他籃球選手最大的不同在於他總是會有備用計畫。假如尼克隊沒有發現他的潛力，他的教育背景也會讓他有所發揮。

1. 解答：d) 他們欣賞有自信的人。

中譯：

為什麼人們深受林書豪謙遜的態度所吸引？

a) 他們喜歡傾聽別人。

b) 他們喜歡自大的人。

c) 他們欣賞他的經驗。

d) 他們欣賞有自信的人。

題解：由文章中所列的第二點可知，人們被林書豪的自信感吸引，而這份自信來自於謙虛的態度。

2. 解答：c) 他擁有極優秀的教育背景。

中譯：

根據本文，為什麼林書豪跟其他選手不同？

a) 他從小就立定人生的志向。

b) 他因辛勤工作備受讚賞。

c) 他擁有極優秀的教育背景。

d) 他成為他所屬球隊的資產。

題解：根據文中第五點可知，他的教育背景使他的人生有更寬廣的路可選擇，故答案選 c) 最恰當。

3. 解答：b) 你的同事

中譯：

在文章內容中，"peers" 這個字的意思是什麼？

a) 你的老闆

b) 你的同事

c) 你的家人

d) 你的朋友們

題解：由文章第四點的前後文可推知，peers 的意思在此指的是同儕或同事，故答案選 b)。

Lady Gaga's Incredible Outfits
女神卡卡的驚人裝扮

07

閱讀重點

本篇文章是討論女神卡卡（Lady Gaga）的驚人裝扮（incredible outfit），和背後的隱藏含意，其閱讀重點如下：

① 她對自己驚人裝扮的解釋
② 此服裝的保存和處理

文章閱讀

Lady Gaga's Incredible Outfits

When Lady Gaga wore a raw meat dress at the 2010 MTV Video Music Awards, she was criticized by animal **protection** groups. She explained following the awards **ceremony** that the dress was a statement about the need to **fight** for what you believe in. "If we don't stand up for what we believe in and if we don't fight for our rights, pretty soon we're going to have as much right as the meat on our own bones. And, I'm not a piece of meat," she said.

Fernandez, the dress designer, said it would be put in an **archive** with her other dresses. To help the dress keep its shape and appearance, it would be preserved and made into a type of jerky before being archived.

The meat dress was frozen after being on TV twice. It was treated with bleach to kill bacteria, and was dyed dark red after it was preserved to make it look the same as when it was first worn. However, after the preservation there were pieces of beef left that were not included in the **reworked** dress.

🔵 學習焦點 ·····································

女神卡卡因反對美國軍方對同志的政策，在出席 MTV 音樂獎頒獎典禮穿著一件驚嚇指數破表的生肉裝，引起諸多話題及保育人士的抗議。

① 第一句點出生肉服裝備受保育團體的批評 "...she was criticized by animal protection groups."；女神卡卡旋即解釋，服裝代表的是捍衛自己的信仰，否則人將如同行屍走肉般，毫無主控權 "...we're going to have as much right as the meat on our own bones."。

② 第二段說明這件服裝的後續處理 "...would be put in an archive with her other dresses."（將會和其他服裝一樣歸檔保存）；同時為了保存外觀，它將會被製成肉乾的形式（made into a type of jerky）。

③ 第三段解釋保存服裝的過程：先用漂白劑殺菌（treated with bleach to kill bacteria），再染成暗紅色（dyed dark red），以便如第一次穿時看起來一

樣（"...look the same as when it was first worn."）。唯一不同處，是少掉幾片牛肉。

語言知識補充站 ••

★ Vocabulary

* protection：【名詞】保護

When Lady Gaga / wore a raw meat dress / at the 2010 MTV Video Music Awards, / she / was criticized by animal protection groups.
當女神卡卡 / 穿一件生肉服裝 / 在 2010 年 MTV 音樂大獎 / 她 / 被動物保育團體批評

* ceremony：【名詞】儀式

She / explained / following the awards ceremony / that the dress was a statement / about the need / to fight for what you believe in.
她 / 解釋 / 在頒獎典禮之後 / 這服裝是個聲明 / 必需 / 捍衛自己所信仰的理念

* fight：【動詞】奮鬥；戰鬥

用法：人 + fight for + 事物 / 信念
If we / don't fight for our rights, / pretty soon / we're going to have / as much right as the meat on our own bones.
如果我們 / 不為自己的權利奮鬥 / 很快地 / 我們將擁有 / 等同行屍走肉般的權利

* archive：【動詞】歸檔保存

To help the dress keep its shape and appearance, / it would be preserved / and made into a type of jerky / before being archived
為了維持這套衣服的剪裁和外觀 / 它將作防腐處理 / 並製成肉乾的形式 / 在被歸檔保存前

＊ rework：【動詞】重做，修訂

After the preservation / there were pieces of beef left / that were not included in the reworked dress.

在保存後 / 剩下幾片牛肉 / 沒有被包含在重製的服裝裡

句型：主詞 , 名詞同位語（表示職位、頭銜或身份）, ＋ V

同位語常用來補充說明所提到的主詞，讓讀者掌握更多資訊，例如人物的身分，同位語前後都要加逗點，置於主詞與動詞之間。

Fernandez, <u>the dress designer</u>, said it would be put in an archive with her other dresses.

同位語 the dress designer，表示主詞 Fernandez 的身份，說明 Fernandez 是服裝的設計師。

● 摘要與測驗重點提示 ●●●

★ 閱讀要項

本篇文章須要注意的重點如下：

① 描述對象：Lady Gaga, her meat dress
② 描述重點：the need to fight for what you believe in, the dress preservation process

① 說明為了什麼而奮鬥：人 + fight for + 事物 / 信念
② 說明主詞的同位語用法：主詞,（名詞同位語）, + V用來補充說此句的主詞。

★ 測驗重點

本文的重點資訊在於女神卡卡的生肉服裝所代表的意義和保存過程。

練習題

1. Why did Lady Gaga want to wear the meat dress?

a) She wanted to make people angry.

b) She wanted to encourage people to stand up for their beliefs.

c) She entered a design competition.

d) She was advertising a new recipe.

2. Which is not included in the preservation process of the meat dress?

a) It was frozen.

b) It was treated with bleach.

c) It was dyed red.

d) It was cooked.

3. What will happen to the meat dress after preservation?

a) It will be eaten.

b) It will be conserved together with other outfits.

c) It will be donated to charity.

d) It will be displayed in a museum.

The Lady Gaga Phenomenon

Known for her amazing clothes, stage presence and advocacy for gay rights, "Lady Gaga" is a worldwide phenomenon.

The famous blond singer is actually a natural brunette born Stefani Joanne Angelina Germanotta in New York City.

Lady Gaga started as a songwriter. She wrote songs for Britney Spears and The Pussycat Dolls while establishing herself as a performer in underground clubs in New York. At the same time, Lady Gaga also wrote songs for her first album *The Fame*, which reflects her inspiration, lifestyle, and personality. The album reached number one in several countries and earned her five Grammys.

She has now sold more than 23 million albums worldwide and is listed among the 100 most important people. Even if you are not a fan of Lady Gaga, you have to agree that she is a real artist writing her own music.

Lady Gaga's Incredible Outfits 女神卡卡的驚人裝扮 焦點特寫篇

7

1. Which does NOT contribute to the Lady Gaga phenomenon?

a) Her age

b) Her fashion sense

c) Her musical ability

d) Her fans

2. How did Lady Gaga start her career?

a) She wrote her first album.

b) She was in The Pussycat Dolls.

c) She was a songwriter.

d) She went to New York.

3. What is true about the album *The Fame*?

a) It is her first album.

b) It won four Grammys.

c) Lady Gaga wrote it for Britney Spears.

d) It was not popular.

文章閱讀 翻譯與題解

● 文章翻譯 ••

女神卡卡的驚人裝扮

　　女神卡卡在 2010 年度 MTV 音樂大獎頒獎典禮上，穿著生肉裝登場時，就備受保護動物團體的批評。頒典禮結束後，她隨即解釋道：這樣的穿著是在表達人們必須捍衛自己的信仰。她說道：「如果我們不維護我們的信念、不捍衛自己的權益，很快地，我們就會如同行屍走肉般毫無自主權。而我並非麻木不仁。」

　　這套服裝的設計師—費南戴茲說：「這套衣服會和她其他的服裝一併收藏。」為了保持這套衣服的剪裁和外觀，在它被歸檔收藏前必需經過防腐處理，製成類似肉乾的形式。

　　這套生肉裝上過電視兩次後就被冷凍起來。先用漂白水殺菌，防腐處理後，再染上深紅色，讓它看來就像第一次穿出來的時候一樣。然而，經過這些處理之後，重新加工的生肉裝，仍有幾片牛肉會流失掉。

● 題解 ••

1. 解答：b) 她想激勵人們維護自己的信念。

中譯：

為何女神卡卡想穿生肉裝？

a) 她想激怒眾人。

b) 她想激勵人們維護自己的信念。

c) 她參加了一場設計競賽。

d) 她在替一份新食譜打廣告。

7

題解：由本文第一段的說明可知，卡卡希望藉生肉裝告訴人們要捍衛自己的價值觀和權益，故答案選 b)。

2. 解答：d) 要烹調。

中譯：

下列哪一項不包括在保存生肉裝的程序當中？

a) 要冷凍。

b) 用漂白水處理。

c) 染上紅色。

d) 要烹調。

題解：根據文章第二和第三段的內容可知，選項 d) 不包含在保存程序中。

3. 解答：b) 它將會與其他裝扮一起被收藏。

中譯：

經過防腐處理的生肉裝會有什麼狀況？

a) 它會被吃掉。

b) 它將會與其他服裝一起被收藏。

c) 它會被捐給慈善團體。

d) 它會被放在博物館展示。

題解：由文章第二段設計師的話可推知，它會跟卡卡其他裝扮一樣被收藏著。

女神卡卡現象

　　卡卡以驚世駭俗的穿著、舞台效果、並為同志權利發聲而聞名，「女神卡卡」已經成為風靡全球的現象。

　　這位有名的金髮歌手，實際上天生的頭髮是深褐色，本名是史戴芬妮‧瓊安‧安潔莉納‧潔曼諾塔，出生於紐約市。

　　女神卡卡以詞曲創作起家。她曾為小甜甜布蘭妮和小野貓譜曲，並開始在紐約的地下俱樂部演出。同時，她也為個人的首張專輯《超人氣》寫歌，這張專輯反映出她的靈感來源、生活和個性。此專輯讓她在許多國家坐上冠軍寶座並奪得五座葛萊美獎。

　　如今，她的唱片專輯在全球已達到兩千三百萬的銷售佳績，名列一百名最重要的人物之一。即使你不是女神卡卡的粉絲，也必須承認她是一位會自己創作的真正才女。

1. 解答：a) 她的年齡

中譯：

下列哪一項不是促成女神卡卡現象的原因？

a) 她的年齡

b) 她的流行敏銳度

c) 她的音樂造詣

d) 她的粉絲們

題解：由文章內文可知，選項 a) 不是產生卡卡現象的因素之一。

2. 解答：c) 她是一位作曲者。

中譯：

女神卡卡是如何展開她的演藝事業？

a) 她寫出自己的第一張專輯。

b) 她加入小野貓團體。

c) 她是一位作曲者。

d) 她去了紐約。

題解：由文章第二段第一句可知，女神卡卡是以詞曲創作起家，故答案選 c)。

3. 解答：a) 這是她的第一張專輯。

中譯：

下列關於《超人氣》專輯的描述，何者正確？

a) 這是她的第一張專輯。

b) 這張專輯獲得四座葛萊美獎。

c) 是女神卡卡為小甜甜布蘭妮而作的。

d) 這張專輯並不受歡迎。

題解：由文章第二段的內容可推知，選項 a) 的答案正確。

生活教育篇

8

Alternative Sex Education
另類性教育

08

閱讀重點

未成年媽媽（teen mothers）在許多國家都造成嚴重的社會問題，本文以墨西哥為例，敘述該國衛生局用另類的（alternative）方法來改善現況，閱讀重點如下：

① 機器嬰兒的用途及功能陳述。
② 青少年體會身為父母的辛勞。

文章閱讀

Alternative Sex Education

In view of the fact that the **percentage** of teen mothers in the northern part of Mexico is far higher than other regions in the nation, the public health office is introducing a robot baby to educate high school students.

The **robot** baby has several kinds of cries. The students have to **differentiate** the meaning of one cry from another. For example, the baby crying may **represent** hunger, fear or urination, and the students have to choose the right response or the baby will keep on crying.

  <u>After taking care of the robot baby</u>, many students realize how exhausting it is to be a parent, and the **authorities** hope this project will help decrease the rate of teen mothers.

● 學習焦點 ··

「養兒方知父母恩」，讓青少年真正體會當父母的辛苦，方可減少未婚媽媽比率過高的問題。

① 第 一 段 以 "In view of the fact that the percentage of teen mothers in the northern part of Mexico is far higher than other regions..." 點出問題所在 － 未成年媽媽比率過高，要以機器嬰兒來解決問題。

② 第二段說明機器嬰兒的功用 "The robot baby has several kinds of cries."（機器嬰兒有幾種哭聲），學生必須對不同哭聲做出正確的處理方式，否則哭聲將會持續 "...the students have to choose the right response or the baby will keep on crying."。

③ 第三段承接前一段的文意，說明學生照顧機器嬰兒後，才知道身為人母的辛苦，希望藉此降低青少年的生育率 "...the authorities hope this project will help decrease the rate of teen mothers."。

★ **Vocabulary**

* percentage：【名詞】比率

用法：percentage ＋ of ＋ 人 / 事物

The percentage of teen mothers / in the northern part of Mexico is / far higher than / other regions in the nation.

未成年媽媽的比率 / 在墨西哥的北部 / 遠高過 / 這國家的其他區域

* robot：【名詞】機器人

The robot baby / has / several kinds of cries.

這機器嬰兒 / 有 / 許多種哭聲

* differentiate：【動詞】區別

用法：人 ＋ differentiate ＋ 事物 $_1$ ＋ from ＋ 事物 $_2$

The students / have to / differentiate the meaning of one cry / from another.

學生 / 必須 / 區別一種哭聲的意義 / 與另一個不同

* represent：【動詞】代表

The baby crying / may represent / hunger, fear or urination.

嬰兒哭聲 / 可能代表 / 飢餓、恐懼、或尿尿

* authority：【名詞】官方；當局（複數形式）

The authorities / hope this project / will help decrease / the rate of teen mothers.

當局 / 希望這計畫 / 將有助於減低 / 未成年媽媽的比例

句型：V-ing ... , S + V

此句型以 V-ing 做句首，可以表現動作的連續性或是因果關係，或者是補充說明主詞所作的動作。

After taking care of the robot baby, many students realize how exhausting it is to be a parent.

表示 students 在照顧機器嬰兒後的狀況

After taking care of the robot baby 表示這些學生在照顧了機器嬰兒之後，才體會到當父母的辛苦，前後兩句存在著因果關係。

摘要與測驗重點提示 ···

★ 閱讀要項

本文是依照 4W + 1H 幾項要素來敘述重點：

• who：teen mothers, the authorities
• what：a robot baby
• where：the northern part of Mexico
• why：the percentage of teen mothers in north Mexico is the highest
• how：The students have to choose the right response or the baby will keep on crying.

① 多少百分比的用法：percentage ＋ of ＋ 人 / 事物
② 區別事物：人 ＋ differentiate ＋ 事物 ₁ ＋ from ＋ 事物 ₂
③ 補充說明主詞所做的動作：V-ing..., S ＋ V

★ 測驗重點

本文章的內容中，一開始就強調機器嬰兒是用來解決未成年媽媽高比率的問題，是一種另類的性教育。藉由照顧過程中產生的疲憊感，讓學生知道未成年父母並不好當。

練習題

1. What is the purpose of the information?

a) To estimate the birth rate in Mexico

b) To introduce an education training tool

c) To learn how to be good mothers

d) To teach how to lose weight fast

2. Which statement correctly describes the situation in the north of Mexico?

a) The percentage of teen mothers is highest there.

b) The population is aging rapidly.

c) The birth rate is decreasing.

d) The traffic there is very congested.

3. What will happen if students respond to the baby's cries in the wrong way?

a) The baby will become quiet.

b) The baby will speak a word.

c) The baby will keep on crying.

d) The baby will become exhausted.

延伸閱讀 ∙∙

Farewell, Facebook

Even after three weeks, the temptation is still strong. But I'm not giving up. I concentrate on my schoolwork and other activities. Three weeks ago, I logged out of Facebook for the last time. I promised myself I would stop wasting so much time online, and I'm determined to keep that promise.

On my first Facebook-free day, I cleaned my room, did laundry, and finished my homework — all before my 11 a.m. class.

Of course Facebook has many advantages. I could chat with friends whom I rarely saw in person. But I didn't build strong relationships with these people. I just looked at the photos they posted on Facebook and read their comments. A few years ago, kids my age didn't have a computer. They didn't even own a cell phone. Life still worked just fine.

Going a few days without Facebook might not be for everyone, but I recommend giving it a try. It's a great experience — even with the bad feelings.

練習題

1. What is the purpose of this information?

a) To list advantages of using Facebook

b) To introduce a personal viewpoint about social networking services

c) To teach people how to tag pictures on Facebook

d) To tell people how to survive without a computer

2. What did the author do on the first day after logging out of Facebook?

a) He talked to friends from home by phone.

b) He wrote an article on the website.

c) He did some household chores.

d) He went to a class at school.

文章翻譯

另類性教育

　　有鑑於墨西哥北部地區，未成年媽媽的比例高於該國其他地區，公共衛生部門正引進一款機器嬰兒來教育這些高中學子。

　　這款機器嬰兒有數種哭聲。學生們必須學會分辨每種哭聲的訊息。比方說，嬰兒哭鬧可能代表肚子餓、害怕或是尿褲子了，而學生們必需得選擇正確的回應方式，否則嬰兒會繼續哭鬧。

　　許多學生在照顧過機器嬰兒之後，瞭解到為人父母是一件多麼令人筋疲力竭的事情，而當局則希望藉此計畫協助降低未成年媽媽的比例。

題解

1. 解答：b) 介紹一項教育訓練的工具

中譯：

這篇資訊的主旨是什麼？

a) 預估墨西哥的生育率

b) 介紹一項教育訓練的工具

c) 學習如何成為好媽媽

d) 教導人們如何快速減重

題解：由文章第一段關鍵句 "The public health office is introducing a robot baby to educate high school students." 可知，為解決未成年媽媽比例過高的問題，所以引進一項教育訓練的工具，故答案選 b)。

8

2. 解答：a) 那裡未成年媽媽的比例最高。

中譯：

下列哪一個敘述正確描述目前墨西哥北部的狀況？

a) 那裡未成年媽媽的比例最高。

b) 人口正快速老化。

c) 生育率正降低中。

d) 那裡的交通堵塞情形嚴重。

題解：由文章第一段第一句可知，墨西哥北部未成年媽媽的比例較其他方高出許多，故答案選 a) 最恰當。

3. 解答：c) 嬰兒會繼續哭鬧。

中譯：

如果學生以錯誤的方式回應嬰兒的哭聲，會有什麼樣的結果？

a) 嬰兒會安靜下來。

b) 嬰兒會說話。

c) 嬰兒會繼續哭鬧。

d) 嬰兒會筋疲力竭。

題解：由文章的第二段末的關鍵句 "...the students have to choose the right response or the baby will keep on crying." 可知，答案選 c) 最適合。

● 文章翻譯 ···

再會了，臉書

即使過了三週，誘惑仍很強烈。但我不會放棄。我會專注於學校的課業和其他活動。三週前是我最後一次登出臉書，並停止下定決心不要再浪費時間在網路上，而且我會堅守這個承諾。

不上臉書的第一天，我打掃了房間、洗了衣服，也做完功課—全都在上午十一點上課之前。

臉書確實有好處。我可以和許多很少碰面的朋友聊天，但並未因此和這些人建立穩固的友誼。只是看看他們貼在臉書上的照片和留言。幾年前，像我這個年齡的孩子們還沒有電腦呢！他們甚至也沒有手機，生活依然過得很好。

過幾天沒有臉書的生活可能不適合每個人，但我仍推薦一試。即使會有負面的感受，那仍是個很棒的體驗。

題解 ....

1. 解答：b) 提出個人對社群網路服務的觀點

中譯：

這則訊息的主旨為何？

a) 列出使用臉書的好處

b) 提出個人對社群網路服務的觀點

c) 教導人們如何在臉書的照片貼標籤

d) 告訴人們在沒有電腦的狀態下如何生存

題解：由文章中第一人稱（I）的語氣可知，是出於個人觀點說明對於社群網路服務的感受，故答案選 b) 最合理。

2. 解答：c) 他做了家事。

中譯：

作者登出臉書之後的第一天做了什麼事情？

a) 他從家裡打電話與朋友們聊天。

b) 他在網路上發表一篇文章。

c) 他做了家事。

d) 他去學校上課。

題解：由文章第二段可知，作者不上臉書之後，有效率地完成打掃房間、洗衣服等家事（household chores）。故答案選 c)。

Counterfeit Fashion
真假時尚

📖 閱讀重點 ••

本篇是討論消費者心態的文章，指出一般人可能會因為貪小便宜，購買仿冒商品（counterfeit），其閱讀重點如下：

① 購買仿冒品的原因。
② 購買仿冒品的害處。

🌐 文章閱讀 ••

Counterfeit Fashion

Maybe you can't **afford** the real thing or perhaps you think you **deserve** a bargain. So you head off to a street corner to buy a fake handbag.

You get the goods you want and save thousands of dollars.

What's the harm?

There are some reasons why you should rethink your buying concept:

1. Good citizens like you pay taxes <u>while</u> **counterfeiting** is a tax-free business.

2. Terrorists, drug dealers, and crime organizations all **profit** from selling fake products. There is evidence that the bombing of the World Trade Center in 1993 was funded by the sale of counterfeit clothing.

3. Products like fake sunglasses can hurt your eyes because they don't **provide** the same level of UV protection as the real goods.

So what will you do the next time you see some fake goods?

學習焦點 ••

本文先說明購買仿冒品的個人理由,再點出仿冒品的害處。

① 第一句以 "Maybe you can't afford the real thing or perhaps you think you deserve a bargain.",揣測要買仿冒品的兩個原因:或許是無法負擔真品,或許是認為便宜的假貨較划算。

② 引導出購買仿冒品的句子,"So you head off to a street corner to buy a fake handbag."(跑到街角購買假的手提包)。

③ 用 "What's the harm?"(有什麼傷害?)做為文章的轉折,將文章帶入核心重點,提供以下的三個理由,希望讀者可以重新思考自己的購物概念:購買

仿冒品就等於幫助逃漏稅、犯罪組織從販賣仿冒品中獲利、仿冒品可能會有害 "...fake sunglasses can hurt your eyes..." （假的太陽眼鏡會損傷視力）。

④ 最後以 "So what will you do the next time you see some fake goods?"，留給讀者省思的空間。

🌐 語言知識補充站 ••

★ Vocabulary

＊ afford：【動詞】買得起；負擔得起
用法：人 ＋ afford ＋ 事物
Maybe / you can't afford / the real thing.
或許 / 你無法負擔 / 真品

＊ deserve：【動詞】值得；應受
用法：人 ＋ deserve ＋ 事物
Perhaps you think / you deserve/ a bargain.
或許你認為 / 你應得到 / 便宜的商品

＊ counterfeiting：【名詞】偽造，仿造
Good citizens like you / pay taxes / while / counterfeiting / is a tax-free business.
像你這樣的好市民 / 應該納稅 / 而 / 仿冒 / 是個不用繳稅的生意

＊ profit：【動詞】有益於，獲利
用法：人 / 機構 ＋ profit from ＋ V-ing
Terrorists, drug dealers and crime organizations / all profit from / selling fake products.
恐怖份子、毒販和犯罪組織 / 全部從中獲利 / 販賣仿冒產品

* provide：【動詞】提供

用法：事物 + provide + 服務 / 功能

Fake products / don't provide / the same level of UV protection / as the real goods.

仿冒產品 / 無法提供 / 同樣程度的 UV 保護 / 如同真實產品

★ Sentence Pattern

句型：$S_1 + V_1 + while + S_2 + V_2$

while 在這裡解釋為「然而」，所帶出的子句是表示與前面的主要子句（$S_1 + V_1$），有互相對比的關係。

Good citizens like you pay taxes <u>while counterfeiting is a tax-free business</u>.

表示對比的關係：好市民要納稅但仿冒是不用繳稅的。

摘要與測驗重點提示 ···

★ 閱讀要項

本篇文章須要注意的重點如下：

① 錯誤或需要規勸的消費行為：buy a fake product
① 行為動機或理由：can't afford the real thing, save thousands of dollars
③ 錯誤消費行為的後果：Counterfeiting is a tax-free business, is connected to terrorist activities, and may harm your health.

① 說明某人買得起某物：人 + afford + 事物
② 說明某人值得享有某物：人 + deserve + 事物
③ 說明從某種行為中獲利：人 / 機構 + profit from + V-ing

★ 測驗重點

本文章的重點資訊在於購買仿冒品的壞處，原因有三：販賣仿冒品的人不納稅，販賣利益可能拿去資助非法活動，仿冒品對人體有害。

練習題

1. What is the general tone of the article?

a) Optimistic　　　　　　　b) Pessimistic
c) Persuasive　　　　　　　d) Malicious

2. What is the main reason people tend to buy counterfeit goods?

a) Because they provide the same level of professional service

b) Because they cost less

c) Because they are refundable

d) Because they are taxable

3. According to the article, which statement is NOT true?

a) Some fake goods will cause health problems.

b) Some criminal gangs benefit from selling fake goods.

c) Fake goods vendors have to pay tax.

d) Counterfeiting business is involved in terror activities.

Counterfeit Fashion　真假時尚　生活教育篇

Cruelty-Free Products

Before taking your next sip of iced tea, check the label on the bottle because you may be drinking a cupful of cruelty to animals. Some companies do painful and deadly tests on animals. They cause animals to suffer simply to investigate the possible health benefits of their foods and drinks, even though animal testing is not enough to prove that a product is healthy.

If you are opposed to animal testing, you can look for products made by companies that do not test their products or ingredients on animals. The best thing to do is to read the labels of products you buy. You may also search for cruelty-free companies and products on websites. As these products tend to be organic, it's better for you and your family. So please take actions to support companies that are working to promote the development and validation of non-animal methods.

1. What is the purpose of this article?

a) To teach people how to keep animals safe

b) To ask people to use goods that have not been tested on animals

c) To describe the procedures of animal testing

d) To speed up the lawmaking process for animal protection

2. Which is the main reason to choose non-animal tested products?

a) They are less expensive.

b) They contain more nutrients.

c) They are produced in a more humane way.

d) They are labeled more clearly.

3. According to the article, how can people find non-animal tested products?

a) By reading a survey report

b) By conducting experiments

c) By online searching

d) By visiting food manufacturers

Counterfeit Fashion 真假時尚 生活教育篇

9

文章閱讀 翻譯與題解

文章翻譯

真假時尚

　　也許你買不起真品或是想要撿便宜，於是前往街角買了一個仿冒的手提包。你得到了想要的商品而且省下好幾千塊。那又何妨？

　　以下幾項理由說明了為何該重新思考你的購物觀：

1. 身為優良公民的你乖乖繳稅，而仿冒行為是一項逃稅事業。

2. 恐怖分子、毒販以及犯罪組織都藉由販賣仿冒品獲利。有證據指出1993 年美國世貿中心爆炸案的資金來源即是販買仿冒服飾的收入。

3. 仿冒的太陽眼鏡等商品會傷害你的眼睛，因為它們無法提供如真品一樣的抗 UV 效果。

　　所以，下次看到假貨時你會怎麼做呢？

題解

1. 解答：c) 具說服性質的

中譯：

這篇文章陳述的語氣為何？

a) 正面樂觀的

b) 負面悲觀的

c) 具說服性質的

d) 惡意的

題解：這篇文章主要訴求是告知讀者購買仿冒品背後衍生的問題，試圖說服人們不要去買仿冒品，故答案選 c) 最適合。

2. 解答：b) 因為比較便宜。

中譯：

人們傾向購買仿冒品的主要原因為何？

a) 因為它們提供同等級的專業服務。

b) 因為比較便宜。

c) 因為可以退換貨。

d) 因為它們有課稅。

題解：從本文前三句的關鍵字詞 "can't afford"、 "bargain"、 "save thousands of dollars" 可推知，人們購買仿冒品是因為想省錢，所以答案選 b) 最貼切。

3. 解答：c) 賣仿冒品的小販必須繳稅。

中譯：

根據這篇文章，下列敘述何者為非？

a) 有些仿冒品會造成健康問題。

b) 一些犯罪組織藉由販賣假貨獲利。

c) 賣仿冒品的小販必須繳稅。

d) 仿冒品生意與恐怖活動有關聯。

題解：文章第二段裡提出的第一點觀念就提到 "...counterfeiting is a tax-free business." 「仿冒行為是一項逃稅事業」，故答案 c) 非正確敘述。tax-free 為形容詞「免繳稅的」。

● 文章翻譯 ∙∙

向動物實驗產品說「不」

　　在您喝下一口冰茶前，請檢視瓶子上的商標，因為您可能正在飲用一杯對動物進行殘忍實驗的飲品。有些公司會在動物身上進行痛苦且致命的實驗。這些讓動物們受苦的實驗，單單只是為了研究該食品或飲料可能的保健功效，即便動物實驗不足以證明該產品有益健康。

　　如果您反對動物實驗，您可以尋找無動物實驗的產品或成分。最佳方法是閱讀您所購買商品上的標籤。您也可以上網搜尋無動物實驗的公司和產品。因為這類產品多半是有機產品，對您和家人都有益。所以請多以實際行動支持努力推行和認證無動物實驗機制的企業。

● 題解 ∙∙

1. 解答：b）要求人們使用無經動物實驗的產品。

中譯：

這篇文章的主旨為何？

a）教育人們如何保護動物安全

b）要求人們使用無動物實驗的產品

c）描述動物實驗的步驟

d）加速動物保育法的立法程序

題解：從文章標題關鍵字 "cruelty-free products" 及文章第二段呼籲支持無動物實驗商品和企業的論點可知，答案應選 b)。

2. 解答：c) 它們以較人道的方式生產。

中譯：

選用非動物實驗產品的主要理由是什麼？

a) 它們的價格較便宜。

b) 它們含有較多營養成分。

c) 它們以較人道的方式生產。

d) 它們的商品標示比較清楚。

題解：文章第一段的描述提到，廠商進行殘忍的動物實驗以測試產品，故鼓勵消費者選用無動物實驗的產品，所以故答案選 c)。humane 為形容詞「人道的」。

3. 解答：c) 藉由上網搜尋

中譯：

根據本文，人們可用何種管道找到非動物實驗的產品？

a) 藉由閱讀調查報告可知

b) 藉由實驗

c) 藉由上網搜尋

d) 藉由參訪食品製造廠

題解：由文章第二段第三句的關鍵句 "You may also search for cruelty-free companies and products on websites." 可知，可上網搜尋支持人道實驗的產品和企業，故答案選 c)。

10

Top 5 Regrets of the Dying
人生反思：死前五大遺憾

（10）

閱讀重點

本篇文章是一位長期照護臨終者（the dying）的護理人員，她發現這些走向生命盡頭的病人都有共同的遺憾。其閱讀重點如下：

① 臨終者的心路歷程。
② 最常有的五大遺憾。

文章閱讀

Top 5 Regrets of the Dying

Bronnie Ware, an Australian nurse who provides care for dying patients, has recorded their most common regrets.

She found that people grow a lot when they are **faced** with their own mortality. They experience the emotions of denial, bargaining, anger, remorse, and eventually acceptance. Bronnie Ware asked them about their regrets. What do they wish they had done differently in their lives? Here are the five most common answers:

1. They wish they had stayed true to themselves, **instead of** living the life that others expected of them.
2. They wish they hadn't worked so hard.
   This regret was expressed mainly by men.
3. They wish they had had the courage to **express** their feelings.
   Although some people may get angry or upset when you are honest with them, in the end, honesty leads to better relationships.
4. They wish they had stayed in touch with their friends.
   In the face of death, love and friendship are the most important things.
5. They wish that they had **allowed** themselves to be happier.
   Life is a choice. It is each person's responsibility to lead a life that makes them happy.

 學習焦點

本文先敘述臨終者的心緒變化，再說明五種最常有的憾事。

① 第一句以一位護士 "…who provides care for dying patients, has recorded their most common regrets."（……照顧臨終病患，記錄下他們最常有的憾事）點出本文主旨。
② 第二段導引出病患臨死前的心境變化，也就是任何人面臨失落時，會出現的心理調適階段：denial, bargaining, anger, remorse, and acceptance（否認、討價還價、憤怒、自責、及接受）。
③ 舉出最常有的遺憾，分別為：

"They wish they had stayed true to themselves..."（忠於自我），"They wish they hadn't worked so hard."（沒那麼努力工作），"They wish they had had the courage to express their feelings."（有勇氣表達自我），"They wish they had stayed in touch with their friends."（與朋友保持聯絡），"They wish they had allowed themselves to be happier."（讓自己更快樂）。

語言知識補充站 ···

★ Vocabulary

＊ regret：【名詞】後悔，遺憾
Bronnie Ware, / an Australian nurse / who provides care for dying patients, / has recorded their most common regrets.
Bronnie Ware / 一位澳洲護士 / 提供臨終病患照護 / 記錄他們最常有的憾事

＊ face：【動詞】面對
用法：人 + face / be faced with + 問題 / 情況
She found / that people grow a lot / when they are faced with / their own mortality.
她發現 / 人們成長許多 / 當他們面對 / 自己的死亡

＊ instead of：代替，取代
用法：instead of + 被取代的事物 / V-ing
They / wish they had stayed / true to themselves, / instead of living the life / that others expected of them.
他們 / 希望他們曾保持 / 對自我真實 / 而不是過著一種生活 / 別人期待他們的

＊ express：【動詞】表達
用法：人 + express + 看法 / 感覺；看法 / 感覺 + be expressed by + 人

This regret / was expressed mainly by men.

這類遺憾 / 主要由男性來表達

＊ allow：【動詞】允許

用法：人 $_1$ ＋ allow ＋ 人 $_2$ ＋ to V

They wish / that they had allowed / themselves / to be happier.

他們希望 / 他們曾允許 / 自己 / 更快樂些

★ **Sentence Pattern**

句型：人 ＋ wish(es) ＋ that ＋ S ＋ had ＋ V-pp

這是英文中所謂的「假設語氣」，表示希望過去應該做到，實際上卻沒有發生或實現的事情。

① They wish they had stayed true to themselves, instead of living the life that others expected of them.

　希望過去有忠於自我，但實際上卻沒有做到。

② They wish they had stayed in touch with their friends.

　希望有和朋友保持聯繫，但實際上卻沒有做到。

● 摘要與測驗重點提示 ●●●●●●●●●●●●●●●●●●●●●●●●●●●●●●●●●●●●

★ 閱讀要項

本篇文章須要注意的重點如下：

① 描述對象：dying patients

② 描述的狀況：their most common regrets

① 面對某種問題或情況：人 + face / be faced with + 問題 / 情況
② 說明被取代的事情：instead of + 被取代的事物 / V-ing
③ 允許他人做某事：人₁ + allow + 人₂ + to V

① 面對某種問題或情況：人 + face / be faced with + 問題 / 情況
② 說明被取代的事情：instead of + 被取代的事物 / V-ing
③ 允許他人做某事：人 $_1$ + allow + 人 $_2$ + to V
④ 過去該做到卻沒有實現的事情：人 + wish(es) + that + S + had + V-pp

★ 測驗重點

本文的重點資訊在於臨終病患都會對自己的人生做反思，並表達出共通性很高的幾件憾事。

練習題

1. What did Bonnie find after taking care of dying patients?

a) That they think very differently

b) That they will not change their minds

c) That they expressed similar opinions about their lives

d) That they have the courage to live a life true to themselves

2. What was the most common life regret for men?

a) They never chose happiness.

b) They did not have the courage to express their feelings.

c) They never contacted their friends.

d) They spent a lot of time on work.

3. What is suggested in this article?

a) People can choose the way they live their lives.

b) People realize health brings freedom.

c) People experience a variety of emotions when they get sick.

d) People should receive hospice care before dying.

How to Measure the Level of Happiness

A lot of research has revealed that there is no direct relation between money and human well-being. If material wealth is not the most important ingredient for a happy life, then what is it? Here are some suggestions:

1. Positive attitudes: People who are optimistic, kind, forgiving, and grateful tend to have an abundance of happy experiences and happy lives.

2. More self-determination: People who have good education, health care, and other economic assets cannot enjoy happy lives if they cannot pursue their own dreams.

3. Close relationships: Those individuals who are supported by intimate friendships are much likelier to say they are very happy.

If you want to be happy, recognize that happiness is a product of the way you think and behave rather than your finances. Being grateful for what you already have is a good start. We are the captains of our ship and the authors of the book of our lives. Let's make it happen.

1. What is the purpose of this article?

a) To teach people how to sail a ship

b) To show people how to earn a fortune

c) To analyze the relationship between money and well-being

d) To recommend ways to stay happy

2. Which is the main characteristic of a self-determined person?

a) Well-educated

b) Rich and famous

c) Pursuing one's dreams

d) Negative

● 文章翻譯 ··

人生反思：死前五大遺憾

一位從事病患安寧照顧的澳洲護士—布蘭妮‧維爾（Bronnie Ware）記錄了臨終病患普遍易感懊悔之事。

她發現當人們意識到自己的生命將走到盡頭，必須面對死亡時，人會成長許多！他們會經歷否認、討價還價、憤怒、自責，到終究仍須接受事實等情緒。

布蘭妮‧維爾（Bronnie Ware）詢問他們關於讓自己感到懊悔的事情。有哪些事情他們希望在人生中可以不同的方式重來？以下是五項最普遍的回答：

1. 他們希望可以忠於自我，而非活在別人的期待下。
2. 他們希望自己不是那麼努力工作。
   主要多由男性發出這樣的感慨。
3. 他們希望過去能夠有勇氣表達自己的情感。
   儘管有些人你對他說實話，他會感到憤怒或沮喪，但最終，真實誠懇才會帶來較佳的人際關係。
4. 他們會希望自己能多和朋友保持聯絡。
   臨終之際，愛和友誼是最重要的。
5. 他們希望讓自己過著更快樂的人生。
   人生就是一項選擇，讓自己度過愉快的一生是每個人的責任。

10

題解 ••

1. 解答：c) 病患們表達了相似的人生見解。

中譯：

布蘭妮在照顧臨終病患時發現了什麼？

a) 每個病患的想法都非常不一樣。

b) 病患不會改變心意。

c) 病患們表達了相似的人生見解。

d) 他們有勇氣過著忠於自己的人生。

題解：有本文第一和第二段內容可推知，紀錄病患們易感懊悔之事，呈現他們有相似的人生見解，故答案選 c)。

2. 解答：d) 他們花了許多時間在工作上。

中譯：

哪一項是男性病患最普遍的人生憾事？

a) 他們不曾選擇愉快過一生。

b) 他們沒有勇氣表達自己的感受。

c) 他們不曾和朋友連絡。

d) 他們花了許多時間在工作上。

題解：由文章所列五點最易感到懊悔之事的第二點可知，主要由男性病患發出這樣的感慨，故選 d)。

3. 解答：a) 人們能夠選擇要以什麼方式過自己的人生。

中譯：

這篇文章提供了什麼樣的啟發？

a) 人們能夠選擇要以什麼方式過自己的人生。

b) 人們體認到健康才會帶來自由。

c) 當人生病的時候會經歷各式各樣的情緒。

d) 人們臨終前應受安寧照護。

題解：本文內容主要論及臨終病患最常有的人生遺憾可知，答案 a) 最適切。

● 文章翻譯 ……………………………………………………………………

如何衡量幸福的程度

　　許多研究發現金錢和人的幸福感沒有直接的關聯。如果說物質財富不是構成快樂人生最重要的因素，那會是什麼呢？以下有一些建議：

1. 正向的態度：擁有樂觀、和善、寬容、愉悅個性的人較易於享有許多愉快的經驗和快樂的生活。

2. 更多自主性：即使受過良好教育、健康照護和享有其他經濟上有利條件的人，如果不能追逐自己的夢想，他們也無法享受到快樂的人生。

3. 親密的關係：能有親密友伴支持的人，較有可能會說他們過得非常幸福。

　　如果你想獲得快樂，請認清：幸福是你思考和行為下的產物，而非決定於你的財力。心存感恩，珍惜已經擁有的是個美好的開始。我們是自己的掌舵者，也是自己的人生之書的作者。讓我們一起實現快樂人生吧！

1. 解答：d) 介紹保持快樂的方法

中譯：

本文的主旨為何？

a) 教導人們如何駕船

b) 告訴人們如何謀求財富

c) 分析金錢和幸福感間的關係

d) 介紹保持快樂的方法

題解：由文章內容可知，本文所列的三點建議都是在提供擁有幸福人生的方向，故答案選 d)。

2. 解答：c) 會追求自己的夢想

中譯：

下列哪一項是一個擁有自主性的人所具備的主要特點？

a) 受過良好的教育

b) 富裕且知名

c) 會追求自己的夢想

d) 負面的

題解：由文章中的第三點可知，擁有自主性的人會去追逐自己的夢想，故答案選 c) 最恰當。

11

How to Become Rich by Doing What Rich People Do

向有錢人看齊

📖 閱讀重點 ....

一般人對於有錢人的生活及如何致富（how the rich got that way）都會感到好奇，本文告訴大家只要遵守幾項原則（principles）就是好的開始，閱讀重點如下：

① 一般大眾對於有錢人的遐想。
② 遵守五項原則，向有錢人看齊。

🌐 文章閱讀 ....

How to Become Rich by Doing What Rich People Do

    People tend to have strange ideas about how the rich got that way and how they live. For every rich person seeming to live a carefree life, many more live **frugally**. If you want to join them, following these **principles** will be a great start.

    1. **Delay gratification.** Allow some time to decide <u>whether you truly need something</u>, and then shop around for the best deal.

2. **Live below your means.** Devise a personal financial plan for your family and you will give yourself an opportunity to become rich.

3. **Pay cash when making purchases.** You will tend to spend less than when using a credit card.

4. **Buy on sale.** Check the weekly sales adverts and buy furniture, clothes and jewelry as rich people do.

5. **Save and invest.** Save at least 15 percent of your annual income and invest wisely. Make money a priority in your life and you will eventually learn the secrets of the rich.

● 學習焦點 ....

本文先點出大家對於富裕這件事的看法，以引起讀者對於想加入有錢人行列的慾望，再列舉五項有助於累積財富的好習慣。

① 第一段說明一般人以為有錢人過著無憂無慮的生活（live a carefree life），實則較多的富人是很簡樸的（...many more live frugally.），接著列出五點致富原則。

② "Delay gratification"（延遲享樂）：思考你是否真需要某件東西（whether you truly need something），答案是肯定時，也要尋找最划算的價錢（best deal）。

③ "Live below your means."（量入為出）：為自己及家人做理財規畫（Devise a personal financial plan for your family...），才有致富的機會。

④ "Pay cash when making purchases." （購物時付現）：付現會比使用信用卡花費更少（tend to spend less）。

⑤ "Buy on sale." （特價時再買東西）查詢每週的特價廣告（Check the weekly sales adverts.），就能像富人般買家具、衣服、珠寶。

⑥ "Save and invest." （儲蓄並投資）：養成存錢的習慣，並明智地投資，把金錢變成人生的優先考慮（Make money a priority in your life.），最終你會學到致富的祕訣。

語言知識補充站 ···

★ Vocabulary

＊ frugally：【修飾詞】節儉地；儉樸地

For every rich person / seeming to live a carefree life, / many more live frugally.

對每位有錢人來說 / 似乎過著無憂無慮的生活 / 更多的富人是節儉地度日

＊ principle：【名詞】原則

If you / want to join them, / following these principles / will be a great start.

如果你 / 要加入他們 / 遵循這些原則 / 將會是個好的開始

＊ devise：【動詞】設計；規畫

Devise a personal financial plan / for your family / and you will give yourself an opportunity / to become rich.

規畫個人理財方案 / 為你的家人 / 而你將給自己一個機會 / 致富

＊ priority：【名詞】優先

用法：人 ＋ make ＋ 事物 ＋ a priority

Make money a priority / in your life / and you will eventually learn / the secrets of the rich.

將金錢視為人生的優先考慮 / 在一生裡 / 你最終將學會 / 有錢人的祕訣

＊與理財有關的常見字彙：

financial（財務的）、cash（現金）、credit card（信用卡）、save（儲蓄）、invest（投資）、means（財力）、income（收入）

★ Sentence Pattern

句型：whether ＋ S ＋ V（是否）

本句型是表示對某件事情不確定或提出疑問；whether 所引導的句子可以作為主詞或受詞。

Allow some time to decide <u>whether you truly need something</u>, and then shop around for the best deal.

表示對於自己真正需要的物品需要一些時間確認，然後再以最划算的價格去購買。

摘要與測驗重點提示 ●●

★ 閱讀要項

本篇文章須要注意的重點如下：

① 描述對象：people who want to be rich（想要變有錢的人）
② 敘述重點：five principles to become the rich 致富的五個原則

① 說明把某件事當成優先考慮：人 ＋ make ＋ 事物 ＋ a priority
② 理財常見字彙：financial, cash, credit card, save, invest, means, income

★ 測驗重點

本文的重點資訊在於如何掌握致富的五項要點。

練習題

1. What is the purpose of this article?

a) To tell you how nice it is to be rich

b) To teach you how to invest in stocks

c) To teach you how to think and act like the rich

d) To tell you how to find the best deal

2. The word "frugally" here is closest in meaning to

a) Carefully

b) Generously

c) Happily

d) Scarily

3. Which of these is NOT a piece of advice from the article?

a) Use credit cards

b) Go to sales

c) Wait before buying

d) Buy only as much as you need

11

The Difference Between Income and Wealth

A large income doesn't always mean you are wealthy; people on a decent income still can't afford to dine at premium hotels or restaurants, because they don't understand the strategy that wealthy people use.

Here are two fictional characters that show the difference between income and wealth.

1. Kevin worked as a manager with an annual income of $60,000. He committed to investing at least 10% of his income, and lived in a small three-bedroom house with his family.  He paid off the mortgage a few years ago. His children attended public schools. When they grew up and needed cars, he bought used cars and paid cash. Kevin and his family may not live lavishly, but they are comfortable and debt free.

2. A highly-skilled doctor, Tom has worked up to a $350,000 yearly salary. Tom's family's expenses, however, the large mortgage, payments on two new cars, private schooling for his children, student loans, club memberships, luxury clothing, and expensive vacations – added up. The costs were equal to his salary. Some years he ended up spending more than he earned. If Tom were to stop working, his family would soon be close to bankruptcy.

These examples are a reminder that the key to accumulating wealth is not to act rich, but to live within one's means.

1. According to the article, what does "wealth" mean?

a) The state of financial success

b) The things you desire

c) The money you earn

d) A big income

2. What did Kevin pay off early?

a) His investment

b) His cars

c) His house

d) His school fees

3. What seems to be Tom's problem?

a) His salary is too low.

b) He spends too little.

c) He sometimes spends more than he earns.

d) His children are at private schools.

How to Become Rich by Doing What Rich People Do　向有錢人看齊　生活教育篇

11

文章閱讀 翻譯與題解

● 文章翻譯 ···

向有錢人看齊

　　人們常對富有的人如何累積到現有的財富，且過著富裕的生活懷有奇想。每個有錢人好像都可以無憂無慮的過一生，但其實大部份的有錢人過著儉約的生活。如果你想加入他們的行列，照著下列原則行事將會是個好的開始：

1. 延遲享樂。留些時間決定你是否真的需要某物，然後再找尋最划算的方案。
2. 量入為出。為你的家庭進行個人理財規劃，你就有機會致富。
3. 買東西時盡量付現。如此一來，會比刷信用卡少花些錢。
4. 趁打折時購物。查詢每週特價廣告，就可以像有錢人一樣買家具、衣服和珠寶。
5. 儲蓄並投資。至少儲蓄年收入的百分之十五，並明智的投資。讓金錢成為人生中的優先考量，最終你會習得致富的祕訣。

● 題解 ···

1. 解答：c) 教你如何像富人一樣思考，像個有錢人

中譯：

本文的主旨是什麼？

a) 告訴你成為有錢人是件多麼棒的事

b) 教你如何投資股票

c) 教你如何像富人一樣思考，像個有錢人

d) 告訴你如何找到最划算的方案

題解：由文章內容可知，本文主旨在說明，如何學習有錢人，讓自己有朝一日也成為富人一族，故答案選 c)。

2. 解答：a) 小心謹慎地

中譯：

此處「節儉地」這個字的意思與下列何者最接近？

a) 小心謹慎地

b) 大方地

c) 愉快地

d) 提心吊膽地

題解：由文章第一段的內容可知，多數有錢人會謹慎節約地用錢，故答案選 a) 最接近。

3. 解答：a) 多刷信用卡。

中譯：

由本文可知，下列哪項不是文章中所建議的？

a) 多刷信用卡。

b) 趁打折時購物。

c) 買之前先等一等。

d) 只買你所需的分量。

題解：由文章第三點建議可知，買東西時盡量付現，不要用刷卡的方式，故答案選 a)。

收入和財富的差別

　　有大筆收入並不等同於富有，有不錯收入的人，仍負擔不起在高級飯店或餐廳用餐，因為他們不了解富裕者的用錢策略。

　　下面提供兩個虛構人物，說明收入和財富的差別：

1. 凱文（Kevin）擔任公司經理，年收入為 60,000 美元。他自我期許至少要將年收入的百分之十用於投資，而且和家人住在三個房間的小房子。他幾年前還清了所有的抵押借款。他的孩子念的是公立學校。當孩子們長大需要開車時，他買二手車給他們，且用的是付現的方式。凱文（Kevin）和他的孩子們或許過得並不奢華，但他們生活得很自在，而且沒有負債。

2. 湯姆（Tom）是位醫術高明的醫師，年薪已經高達 350,000 美元。他的家庭開銷包含大筆抵押借款、買兩台新車的支出、孩子們念私立學校的費用、學生貸款、俱樂部會費、奢華的服飾、豪華假期的支出等。這些費用大概等於他的薪水。有些時候一年下來，花的錢比他賺的還要多。一旦湯姆（Tom）不工作，他的家庭很快就會瀕臨破產。

　　舉這些例子是在提醒，累積財富的關鍵並不是表現得像個有錢人就可以了，而是要設法在自己財富能力範圍內過活。

1. 解答：a) 理財成功的狀態

中譯：

根據本文的描述，「財富」這個字的意思為何？

a) 理財成功的狀態

b) 你所渴求的事物

c) 你賺到的錢

d) 一大筆收入

題解：由本文內容可知，主要說明財富與收入的差別，而財富所指的是策略地使用和管理你的金錢，故答案選 a)。

2. 解答：c) 他的房子

中譯：

凱文較早清償的是哪一項？

a) 他的投資

b) 他的汽車

c) 他的房子

d) 他的學費

題解：由文章中的第一個例子的關鍵句 "He paid off the mortgage a few years ago." 可知，他最先清償房屋的抵押借款，故答案選 c)。

3. 解答：c) 他有時候花的錢比賺得的多。

中譯：

下列哪一項可能是湯姆（Tom）的問題所在？

a) 他的薪水太低。

b) 他錢花得太少。

c) 他有時候花的錢比賺得的多。

d) 他的孩子念的是私立學校。

題解：由文章的第二個例子可知，湯姆收入可觀，但是家庭開銷龐大，缺乏理財計畫，故答案選 c) 最合理。

12

Behind the Label
名牌背後的真相

閱讀重點

本篇文章主要在揭露那些生產名牌精品的血汗工廠（sweatshops）的事實，其閱讀重點如下：

① 名牌公司藉血汗工廠賺取利潤
② 喚醒消費者的道德意識與良知

文章閱讀

Behind the Label

Take a look into your closet. Any brand-name jeans, shirts, or sweaters? The clothes may be high-quality and sure, they look great, but the companies behind these brands have made a fortune using **sweatshop** labor.

They choose to produce their products in poor countries with weak economies, **partnering** with factories that pay workers, mainly women, very low wages and force them to work up to 20 hours a day. Some of these sweatshops violate child labor laws by employing children as workers.

Many of these products are seemingly made in legitimate "normal" factories, but in order to keep costs down, companies regularly outsource production to illegal sweatshops. The CEOs at the top of the corporations know what's going on. But using sweatshop labor helps them to increase profits and keep stock prices high. That's what they care about most.

So what do you care about? The stock prices of these major companies? Or the women who work hard to support themselves and their families and who deserve to have decent working conditions?

● 學習焦點 ••

在我們身著時尚華服、享受科技用品時,是否有想到製作這些產品的勞工是一群任人宰割的弱勢族群,他們卑微的薪資造就這些財團豐厚的利潤。

① 第一段從邀請讀者檢視家裡的衣櫃,點出文章的主題－製造這些名牌商品的公司可能是藉著剝削血汗工廠的勞工而致富 "...the companies behind these brands have made a fortune using sweatshop labor."。

② 第二段說明血汗工廠的工作情況。他們選擇在經濟落後的窮國("poor countries with weak economies")製造產品,用低薪及超時工作壓榨勞

12

工，甚至違法雇用童工 "...violate child labor laws by employing children as workers."。

③ 第三段則點出這些將產品外包給血汗工廠的公司總裁其實是知道內幕的，但是增加利潤和提高股價（increase profits and keep stock prices high）才是他們最關心的事情。

④ 第四段反問讀者在乎的是什麼？"So what do you care about?" 股價？還是辛苦工作養家的勞工？

🌐 語言知識補充站 ···

★ Vocabulary

* sweatshop：【名詞】血汗工廠
The clothes / may be high-quality / but the companies behind these brands / have made a fortune / using sweatshop labor.
衣服 / 可能是高品質 / 但是這些品牌背後的公司 / 賺了錢 / 使用血汗工廠的勞工

* partner：【動詞】合作；同夥
用法：partner with ＋ 合作對象
They choose to produce their products / in poor countries with weak economies, / partnering with factories / that pay workers, / mainly women, / very low wages.
他們選擇製造自家產品 / 在經濟落後的貧窮國家 / 與工廠合作 / 支付勞工 / 主要是女人 / 非常低的工資

* violate：【動詞】違反；違背
Some of these sweatshops / violate child labor laws / by employing children / as workers.
有些血汗工廠 / 違反童工法規 / 雇用孩童 / 當作勞工

＊ outsource：【動詞】外包

Many of the parts / are made in legitimate "normal" factories, / but in order to keep costs down, / companies regularly outsource production / to illegal sweatshops.

許多零件 / 是由合法「正常」的工廠生產 / 但為了壓低成本 / 公司經常將生產外包 / 給非法的血汗工廠

＊ decent working conditions

指正常合法的工作環境，在美國有所謂的 Decent Working Conditions and Fair Competition Act（正常工作環境及公平競爭法案），就是為了保護勞工免於被剝削及壓榨。

★ Sentence Pattern

句型：S + V, V-ing...

接續在主要子句後面的 Ving 可以表現動作的連續性或是因果關係，或者是補充說明主詞所作的動作。

They choose to produce their products in poor countries with weak economies, partnering with factories that pay workers, mainly women, very low wages.

表示主詞 they 除了選擇（choose）在落後國家生產外，還與血汗工廠合夥；partnering 所帶出的語句就是補充說明前面的動作。

摘要與測驗重點提示 ●●●●●●●●●●●●●●●●●●●●●●●●●●●●●●●●

★ 閱讀要項

本篇文章須要注意的重點如下：

Behind the Label 名牌背後的真相 生活教育篇 12

① 描述對象：sweatshops
② 敘述重點：how the brand-name products are produced
　　　　　　（名牌商品是如何生產的）

★ 常用字彙及句法

① 說明與人合夥：partner with ＋ 合作對象
② 補充說明主詞所作的動作：S ＋ V, V-ing...

★ 測驗重點

本文的重點資訊在於名牌產品背後的勞工剝削狀況。

練習題

1. What is the general tone of the article?

a) Optimistic　　　　　　　　b) Humorous

c) Serious　　　　　　　　　 d) Informal

2. Why do those companies use sweatshops to produce their products?

a) They want to increase their profitability.

b) They want to train the workers.

c) They want to bribe officials in developing countries.

d) They want to go public and trade on the stock market.

3. According to the article, which statement is NOT true?

a) Some fashion products are made by child labor.

b) Consumers are encouraged to buy sweat-free products.

c) A lot of small companies rely heavily on sweatshop labor.

d) Workers in illegal factories struggle to make ends meet.

Eco-Friendly Fashion

Eco-fashion is about making clothes in a way that is environmentally friendly and takes into account the health of consumers and the working conditions of employees in the fashion industry.

The clothes are made from organic materials, such as cotton grown without the use of pesticides. It is forbidden to use harmful chemicals to color fabrics. Eco-friendly clothing is often made from recycled textiles. High-quality pieces of clothing can be made from second-hand clothes and even recycled plastic bottles. Finally, eco-fashion follows the rules of fair trade. That means that the people who make them receive a fair salary and have decent working conditions.

Some people believe that clothes made from organic materials are not as durable and wear out more quickly. In fact, the opposite is true. They are actually more resistant to frequent washing than conventionally made clothes. So although eco-friendly clothes tend to cost more, they may be less expensive in the long-run simply because they last longer.

However, the eco-fashion industry is still in its infancy. David Hieatt, the owner and founder of Hiut Denim says that manufacturers and consumers need to share the responsibility for more sustainable fashion. The answer, he says, is simple: "To consume less as a consumer; to make a better designed product as a manufacturer."

12

1. What material can be made into eco-friendly clothing?

a) Recycled plastic bottles

b) Animal skin and bones

c) Cotton fabric containing pesticide residue

d) Easily worn-out fiber

2. According to the article, which statement is NOT true?

a) Organic clothes are more expensive than conventional clothing.

b) The eco-fashion business is in an early stage of existence.

c) Better designed clothes can help save the earth.

d) Eco-wear manufacturers often use cheap labor.

文章閱讀 翻譯與題解

● 文章翻譯 ....

名牌背後的真相

看看你的衣櫃。有沒有任何一件名牌的牛仔褲、襯衫或是毛衣呢？這些衣服可能的確是高品質，而且想當然爾，看起來還不賴，但這些知名品牌背後的公司，卻靠著壓榨血汗工廠的勞力獲得巨大利潤。

他們選擇到經濟貧窮的國家生產他們的產品，與那些多半雇用女性勞工且薪資低廉，並迫使員工一天至少要工作二十小時的工廠結盟。這些血汗工廠中有些甚至違法雇用童工。

許多這類產品表面上似乎是在合法的「正常」工廠生產，但為了降低成本，公司一般都會再外包給非法的血汗工廠代工。那些大企業的執行長（CEOs）都很清楚他們自己在玩什麼把戲。但利用血汗勞工有助於增加獲利並維持高股價。這才是他們最關心的。

所以，你關心的是什麼呢？是這些大公司的股價嗎？或是那些為了維生和養家活口的婦女？以及那些應該獲得合理工作環境的員工？

● 題解 ....

1. 解答：c）嚴肅的

中譯：

這篇文章普遍使用的語氣為何？

a）樂觀的　　　　　　　　　　b）幽默的

c）嚴肅的　　　　　　　　　　d）非正式的

題解：由文章的標題及內容可知，全文主要在討論血汗工廠的問題，是以嚴肅又帶著批判的口吻談論，故答案選 c)。

2. **解答**：a) 他們希望提高自己的獲利率。

中譯：

為何那些公司要利用血汗工廠生產他們的產品？

a) 他們希望提高自己的獲利率。

b) 他們希望去訓練員工。

c) 他們想賄賂開發中國家的官員。

d) 他們希望公司股票上市並在股票市場交易。

題解：由文章內容可知，那些利用血汗工廠的公司，在乎的是降低成本、提高利潤以抬高股價，故答案選 a)。

3. **解答**：c) 許多小公司非常依賴血汗勞力。

中譯：

根據本文，下列哪項敘述不正確？

a) 有些時尚產品是由童工所生產的。

b) 消費者被鼓勵購買來自非血汗工廠的產品。

c) 許多小公司非常依賴血汗勞力。

d) 在非法工廠工作的勞工努力掙錢才能糊口。

題解：本文所指，會依賴血汗工廠降低成本的公司，多半是大公司採用的策略，故選項 c) 不正確。

● 文章翻譯

環保時尚

環保時尚指的是以對環境友善的方式製造衣物,並關懷顧客的健康,同時考量時尚產業員工的工作。

這些衣服是以有機素材製成,例如棉花的種植過程不使用殺蟲劑。也禁止使用有害的化學藥劑染布。對環境友善的布料通常是由回收的原料織成。高品質的布料可能是由二手的回收布料,以及甚至是由塑膠瓶經處理後製成的。最終,環保時尚也遵照公平交易的規則。指的是製作這些東西的工人能獲得相符的報酬和適宜的工作環境。

有些人會認為有機素材製作的衣服不那麼耐用,且很容易就穿壞了。事實上卻完全相反。它們反而比一般衣服更耐洗。所以,即使對環境友善的衣服可能比較貴一些,但長期來看反而比較便宜,因為他們持久耐用。

然而,環保時尚產業仍只是在萌芽階段。大衛·海特(David Hieatt)─惠特·丹寧公司(Hiut Denim)的擁有者及創辦人說:「製造商和消費者應有責任共同承擔永續時尚的發展。」他說這個解決之道很簡單,就是:「作為一個消費者,消費少一點;作為一個製造商,就要做好一點的設計」。

1. 解答：a) 回收的塑膠瓶

中譯：

哪一種素材可以被製成對環境友善的布料？

a) 回收的塑膠瓶

b) 動物的毛皮和骨頭

c) 有農藥殘留的棉布

d) 容易磨損的纖維

題解：由文章第二段的說明可知，答案選 a) 最恰當。

2. 解答：d) 環保衣著的製造商常使用廉價勞力。

中譯：

根據這篇文章，下列哪項敘述不正確？

a) 有機服飾比一般的衣服還貴。

b) 環保時尚事業還在初期階段。

c) 有較佳設計的衣服，可以幫助拯救地球。

d) 環保衣著的製造商常使用廉價勞力。

題解：根據這篇文章的介紹，環保衣著的製造商也會遵循公平交易規範，保障員工的薪資及工作環境，故選項 d) 的描述不正確。

健康環保篇

13

Fast Food
速食風潮

閱讀重點

本文是說明速食店（fast food restaurants）在台灣風行的現象，其閱讀重點如下：

① 速食店在台灣風行的原因。
② 愛吃速食可能產生的負面影響。

文章閱讀

Fast Food

Fast food restaurants have been **mushrooming** in Taiwan over the past two decades.

These restaurants are **characterized** by speed in both food preparation and customer service, as well as speed in customer eating habits.

Young people are especially attracted by fast food because they like the **atmosphere** in fast food restaurants and they can buy clean food at reasonable prices with good service.

However, fast food contains too many **calories**, which make people gain weight and even cause cardiovascular disease.

In conclusion, people who enjoy fast food must pay careful **attention** to their health.

● 學習焦點 ••

在台灣有多種飲食種類可滿足不同的口味，對青少年而言，速食店無疑是個用餐與社交需求可以同時滿足的好選擇。

① 第一句以 "Fast food restaurants have been mushrooming in Taiwan." 點出文章的主旨－速食店在台灣如雨後春筍般的普及。接著說明這些速食店的特徵 "...speed in both food preparation and customer service, as well as speed in customer eating habits."，包含供餐速度、顧客服務、和用餐速度。

② 第二段簡述速食店吸引人的原因：餐廳氣氛（the atmosphere in fast food restaurants）、合理價格（reasonable prices）以及優質服務（good service）。

③ 第三段承接前一段的文意，說明速食店的負面影響，主要是熱量過高，對健康可能不利："...fast food contains too many calories, which make people gain weight and even cause cardiovascular disease."。

④ 第四段總結，速食愛好者必須小心自己的健康狀況。

＊ mushroom：【動詞】如雨後春筍地湧現

用法：名詞＋ have been mushrooming（表示已經湧現）

Fast food restaurants / have been mushrooming / in Taiwan / over the past two decades.

速食店 / 如雨後春筍地湧現 / 在台灣 / 在過去二十多年來

＊ characterize：【動詞】具有……的特徵，以……作為特徵

用法：人 / 物＋ be 動詞＋ characterized ＋ by ＋ 特徵

These restaurants / are characterized by speed / in both food preparation / and customer service, / as well as speed in customer eating habits.

這些餐廳 / 以速度為特徵 / 準備食物 / 和顧客服務 / 以及顧客進食習慣的速度

＊ atmosphere：【名詞】氣氛，空氣

Young people / are especially attracted by fast food / because they like the atmosphere / in fast food restaurants.

年輕人 / 特別為速食所吸引 / 因為他們喜歡這種氣氛 / 在速食店裡

＊ calorie：【名詞】卡路里

Fast food / contains too many calories, / which make people gain weight / and even cause cardiovascular disease.

速食 / 含有過多的卡路里 / 會使人體重增加 / 且甚至引起心血管疾病

＊ attention：【名詞】注意，專心

用法：人＋ pay attention to ＋ 事物

In conclusion, / people who enjoy fast food / must pay careful attention to their health.

總而言之 / 享受速食的人 / 必須仔細注意他們的健康

句型：$S_1 + V_1 + N$, which $+ S_2 + V_2$

which 所引導的子句主要是補充說明前面的事物，傳達更多資訊、介紹狀況給讀者。

However, fast food contains too many calories, <u>which make people gain weight and even cause cardiovascular disease</u>.

which 所帶出來的子句補充說明前面的事物（calories）：它會使人們增加體重和引起心血管疾病。

摘要與測驗重點提示 ....

★ 閱讀要項

本篇文章須要注意的重點如下：

① 文章主旨：Fast food restaurants have been mushrooming in Taiwan.
② 原因分析：the atmosphere, reasonable prices, and good service
③ 負面影響：Fast food contains too many calories, which make people gain
            weight and even cause cardiovascular disease.

★ 常用字彙及句法

① 某物迅速出現：名詞 + mushroom
② 某事物的特徵：人 / 物 + be 動詞 + characterized + by + 特徵
③ 表示專心在某件事上面：人 + pay attention to + 事物

本文章的重點資訊是包括消費者喜愛速食的原因，以及速食對身體會造成何種影響。

練習題

1. Which is NOT a feature of fast food restaurants?

a) Clean food at reasonable prices

b) Efficient food preparation

c) Attractive atmosphere

d) Less processed food

2. The word "mushrooming" in line 1 is closest in meaning to?

a) challenging

b) flourishing

c) decreasing

d) constructing

3. What does the article indicate?

a) Young people should eat food fast.

b) Customer service needs improving in fast food restaurants.

c) People should not eat too much fast food.

d) Fast food restaurants should lower food prices.

Bottled Water

People drink more bottled water every year, mainly because they think it is safer or better than tap water. They spend hundreds or thousands of dollars more every year for water in a plastic bottle than they would for the H_2O flowing from their taps. Bottled water generally is no cleaner, safer, or healthier than tap water. In fact, about 40 percent of bottled water is bottled tap water.

Furthermore, the production of bottled water causes many public health and environmental problems. Making the plastic bottles uses energy and produces dangerous chemicals. Transporting the bottled water across hundreds or thousands of miles releases carbon dioxide into the air, complicating our efforts to fight global climate change. And finally, the empty bottles end up in huge piles of trash. Choosing tap water over bottled water is better for your health, your money, and the environment.

1. What is indicated in this article?

a) Bottled water contains a lot of nutrients.

b) Bottled water is environmentally friendly.

c) Almost half of bottled water is from tap water.

d) The cost of bottled water is the same as tap water.

2. According to the article, why do people consume more bottled water?

a) It is cheap.

b) People think it is better than tap water.

c) It is available everywhere.

d) It is easy to carry.

3. What is NOT one of bottled water's contributions to global warming?

a) The production of bottled water

b) The recycling of used bottles

c) The delivery of bottled water

d) The piling up of bottles as trash

● 文章翻譯 ··

速食風潮

　　速食餐廳過去二十年間在台灣如雨後春筍般湧現。這些餐廳的特色是供餐和顧客服務的速度，就連顧客的用餐也很迅速。

　　年輕人特別受速食吸引的原因是他們喜歡速食餐廳的氣氛，而且他們可以用合理的價格，買到衛生的食物和親切的服務。

　　然而，速食含有過高的卡路里，會讓人發胖，甚至導致心血管疾病。總而言之，喜愛吃速食的人必須特別注意健康。

🏮 題解 ··

1. 解答：d) 較少加工過的食品

中譯：

下列哪一項不是速食餐廳的特色？

a) 價格合理且衛生的食物

b) 供餐速度快

c) 吸引人的氣氛

d) 較少加工過的食品

題解：根據文章內容可知，只有選項 d) 的 less processed food（較少加工過的食品）不是速食餐廳的特色。

2. 解答：b) 迅速湧現

中譯：

文章第一行中 "mushrooming" 這個字的意思最接近於？

a) 挑戰

b) 迅速湧現

c) 減少

d) 建構

題解：依據文章第一段可推知，該字表示「迅速湧現、發展」的意思，故答案選 b) 最相近。

3. 解答：c) 人們不應該吃太多速食。

中譯：

這篇文章暗示了什麼？

a) 年輕人應該吃速食。

b) 速食餐廳的顧客服務有待改進。

c) 人們不應該吃太多速食。

d) 速食餐廳應該降低食物的價格。

題解：文章最後兩句提到速食熱量高，並提醒吃速食的人要注意健康，應有所節制，所以 c) 是正確選項。

● 文章翻譯

瓶裝水的迷思

　　每年人們飲用越來越多瓶裝水，主要是因為他們認為瓶裝水比自來水安全。人們每年在塑膠瓶裝水上的花費較過去的自來水多出數百甚至數千元。一般而言，瓶裝水其實沒有比自來水乾淨、安全或健康。事實上，有百分之四十的瓶裝水不過是瓶裝的自來水而已。

　　瓶裝水的生產甚至引起許多公共衛生和環境問題。製造塑膠瓶不但耗費能源且會產生有毒的化學物質。千里迢迢運送這些瓶裝水更增加空氣中二氧化碳的排放，讓對抗全球氣候變遷的工作更加艱難。最終空瓶還會變為成堆的垃圾。選擇自來水而非瓶裝水其實更有益於您的健康、荷包和環境。

● 題解

1. 解答：c) 約有半數的瓶裝水是來自自來水。

中譯：

這篇文章中指出了什麼問題？

a) 瓶裝水營養豐富。

b) 瓶裝水是環保的。

c) 約有半數的瓶裝水是來自自來水。

d) 瓶裝水的成本與自來水相同。

題解：關鍵句為第一段最後一句 "about 40 percent of bottled water is bottled tap water."，故答案選 c) 最合理。

2. 解答：b) 人們認為它比自來水好。

中譯：

根據這篇文章，為什麼人們飲用更多的瓶裝水？

a) 它很便宜。

b) 人們認為它比自來水好。

c) 它隨處可得。

d) 它容易攜帶。

題解：關鍵句為全文第一句 "People drink more bottled water every year, mainly because they think it is safer or better than tap water."，故答案選 b) 最恰當。

3. 解答：b) 回收使用過的空瓶

中譯：

下列哪一項不是瓶裝水對全球暖化產生的影響？

a) 瓶裝水的生產

b) 回收使用過的空瓶

c) 瓶裝水的運送

d) 成堆的垃圾空瓶

題解：第二段提到瓶裝水帶來的環境衝擊，但未提到回收工作（recycling），故選 b)。

14

Sleep Deficit
睡眠不足

閱讀重點

人的一生有三分之一的時間都需要睡眠，方能維持正常健康的生活；本文以青少年睡眠不足為主題，閱讀重點如下：

① 充足睡眠的重要性。
② 青少年睡眠不足的兩大主因。

文章閱讀

Sleep Deficit

Most teens need more than 8 hours of sleep each night. The right **amount** of sleep is important for teens <u>who want to do well in exams or play sports without injuring themselves</u>. **Unfortunately**, many teens don't get enough sleep.

There are two main reasons that **contribute** to the lack of sleep in teens. The first is the biological clock. The brain **hormone** which helps people fall asleep is produced later at night in teens than in others. This can make it harder for teens to fall asleep early.

Early start time in school is the second main cause for this sleep deficit. Teens <u>who fall asleep late</u> may still have to get up early for school. That means that high school students often only get 6 to 7 hours of sleep at night.

● 學習焦點 ··

本文是分析青少年睡眠不足的原因，包括生理時鐘（biological clock），及上學的時間太早（early start time in school）。

① 在第一段裡以 "Most teens need more than 8 hours of sleep each night... Unfortunately, many teens don't get enough sleep." 點出文章的主旨——大多數青少年需要超過八小時的睡眠，但是，卻無法做到。

② 第二段說明沒有八小時睡眠的原因，主要有兩方面，一為生理時鐘："The brain hormone which helps people fall asleep is produced later at night in teens than in others."（青少年大腦內幫助入睡的賀爾蒙分泌時間較其他人晚。）

③ 第三段承接前一段的文意，說明第二個原因是提早到校的影響："Early start time in school is the second main cause for this sleep deficit."，晚睡的青少年仍必須早起上學，所以中學學生經常只有六到七小時的夜間睡眠。

★ **Vocabulary**

＊ deficit：【名詞】缺少，缺乏

Early start time in school / is / the second main cause / for this sleep deficit.
很早的上課時間 / 是 / 第二個主要因素 / 造成睡眠不足

＊ amount：【名詞】總數，數量

用法：the amount of ＋ 事 / 物

The right amount of sleep / is important / for teens / who want to do well in exams / or play sports without injuring themselves.
正確睡眠時數 / 是重要的 / 對青少年 / 想要考好成績 / 或不受運動傷害

＊ unfortunately：【修飾語】不幸地

Unfortunately, / many teens / don't get enough sleep.
不幸地 / 許多青少年 / 沒有充足睡眠

＊ contribute：【動詞】貢獻，造成

用法：人 / 事 / 物 ＋ contribute ＋ to ＋ 結果 / 影響

There are two main reasons / that contribute to / the lack of sleep of teens.
兩個主要原因 / 造成 / 青少年缺乏睡眠

＊ hormone：【名詞】賀爾蒙

The brain hormone / which helps people fall asleep / is produced later at night / in teens / than in others.
大腦賀爾蒙 / 幫助人們入睡 / 夜間較晚時產生 / 青少年體內 / 比其他人

14

句型：$S_1 + V_1 + N + ($ who $+ S_2 + V_2)$ 或 $S_1 + ($ who $+ S_2 + V_2) + V_1$

who 所引導的子句主要是修飾前面談到的人物，指出跟此人物有關的特定資訊或狀況。

① The right amount of sleep is important for teens <u>who want to do well in exams or play sports without injuring themselves.</u>

who 是指前面的青少年（teens），說明想在課業及運動表現優異的青少年，適量的睡眠對他們十分重要。

② Teens <u>who fall asleep late</u> may still have to get up early for school.

who 是指前面的青少年（teens），說明晚入睡的青少年，仍然必須早起上學。

摘要與測驗重點提示 ••

★ 閱讀要項

本篇文章須要注意的重點如下：

① 文章主題：Many teens don't get enough sleep.
② 原因分析：biological clock and early start time in school

★ 常用字彙及句法

① 某事物的數量：the amount of ＋ 事 / 物
② 造成何種影響：人 / 事 / 物 ＋ contribute ＋ to ＋ 結果 / 影響

本文章的重點資訊是青少年無法睡滿八小時的原因：一是青少年生理時鐘的影響，二是必須早起。

練習題

1. How many hours of sleep is the right amount for teens?

a) 5

b) 6

c) 7

d) 9

2. Why do teens usually fall asleep later than adults?

a) Their sleep hormone is produced later than in adults.

b) They play computer games late at night.

c) They eat more food than adults.

d) They have too much exercise in the daytime.

3. Why do schools also play a role in teens' sleep deficit?

a) Too much homework

b) Early start times in schools

c) Late dismissal at schools

d) Too many extracurricular activities

Sleep Deficit　睡眠不足　健康環保篇

14

Have A Nice Sleep

Adolescents preparing for the upcoming entrance examination sometimes have sleep problems. Here are some suggestions that you can follow to improve the quality of your sleep

- Good sleep habits: These habits should include a regular sleep schedule that involves going to bed and waking up at the same time every day.
- Relaxation: Try to learn some relaxation strategies such as deep breathing or meditation. These strategies can help you relax and feel comfortable while lying in bed.
- Positive thoughts about sleep: Tell yourself "Tonight I'll just relax and rest at bedtime." instead of "I won't be able to sleep tonight."
- Don't be a clock watcher: Watching a clock during the night may make you more anxious and make it even harder for you to fall asleep.

Don't take sleeping pills as the side effects may hurt your health.

1. What is the purpose of this article?

a) To tell people how to live a balanced life

b) To teach students how to prepare exams

c) To recommend tips for a better sleep

d) To guide people how to meditate

2. Which of the following is suggested in the article?

a) A regular daily schedule

b) Negative thoughts

c) Being a clock watcher

d) Prescribed sleeping pills

14

文章閱讀 翻譯與題解

睡眠不足

多數青少年每晚需要八小時以上的睡眠。足夠的睡眠時數，對任何想要考出好成績或避免運動傷害的人而言，都是很重要的。只可惜許多青少年沒有獲得足夠的睡眠。

有兩個主要原因導致青少年睡眠不足。第一項是生理時鐘。青少年大腦內幫助入睡的賀爾蒙分泌的時間會較其他人來得晚，這將使得青少年較難早早入睡。

而上課時間太早是睡眠不足的第二個主因。晚睡的青少年仍需早起上學，那意味著高中生晚上通常只睡六到七小時。

● 題解

1. 解答：d) 九小時
中譯：
多少小時的睡眠對青少年而言是足夠的？
a) 五小時
b) 六小時
c) 七小時
d) 九小時
題解：文章第一段第一句即提到 "Most teens need more than 8 hours of sleep each night." 指出青少年需要八小時以上的睡眠，故答案選 d) 最恰當。

2. 解答：a) 他們睡眠賀爾蒙分泌的時間較成年人稍晚。

中譯：

為什麼青少年通常較成年人晚入眠？

a) 他們睡眠賀爾蒙分泌的時間較成年人稍晚。

b) 他們玩電玩到深夜。

c) 他們比成年人吃更多食物。

d) 他們白天過度運動。

題解：由文章第二段第三句的關鍵句 "The brain hormone which helps people fall asleep is produced later at night in teens than in others." 可知，原因和青少年的賀爾蒙（hormones）分泌有關係，所以答案選 a) 最合理。

3. 解答：上課時間很早

中譯：

為什麼學校也是影響青少年睡眠不足的原因？

a) 太多回家作業

b) 上課時間很早

c) 學校晚下課

d) 過多的課外活動

題解：關鍵句為第三段第一句 "Early start times in schools are the second main cause for this sleep deficit."，由此可知答案選 b) 最適當。

14

延伸閱讀 翻譯與題解

● 文章翻譯 ⋯⋯⋯⋯⋯⋯⋯⋯⋯⋯⋯⋯⋯⋯⋯⋯⋯⋯⋯⋯⋯⋯⋯⋯⋯⋯⋯⋯⋯

向失眠道晚安

青少年在準備即將來臨的入學考試時偶爾會有睡眠問題。下面有幾項改善睡眠品質的建議可供你參考：

- 良好的睡眠習慣：養成規律的睡眠習慣，每天在固定時間就寢和起床。
- 放鬆：試著學習一些放鬆的技巧，像是深呼吸或是冥想。這些技巧能幫助你在床上時感到舒服放鬆。
- 對睡眠的正向思考：告訴自己「今晚我將放鬆、上床好好休息」，而非「我今晚將無法入眠」。
- 不要當個守夜人：在夜裡盯著時鐘可能會使你更加緊張，且會使你更難以入眠。

請勿服用安眠藥，其作用會傷害你的健康。

● 題解 ⋯⋯⋯⋯⋯⋯⋯⋯⋯⋯⋯⋯⋯⋯⋯⋯⋯⋯⋯⋯⋯⋯⋯⋯⋯⋯⋯⋯⋯⋯⋯⋯

1. 解答：c) 提供改善睡眠的建議

中譯：

這篇文章的主旨為何？

a) 告訴人們如何過著均衡的生活

b) 教導學生如何準備考試

c) 提供改善睡眠的建議

d) 引導人們如何冥想

題解：由文章第二句為關鍵句 "Here are some suggestions that you can follow to improve the quality of your sleep..." 可知，本文提供的是幫助人們入眠的技巧，故選 c)。

2. 解答：a) 每日固定作息

中譯：

下列哪一項是文章中所建議的方式？

a) 每日固定作息

b) 負面思考

c) 當個不時查看時間的人

d) 處方的安眠藥

題解：由文章第一點建議 "Good sleep habits" 可知，養成固定的就寢和起床習慣有助改善睡眠，故答案選 a)。

15

Benefits of Green Tea
綠茶的保健妙用

15

🔵 閱讀重點 ••

本篇文章介紹在中國和日本廣受流行的綠茶（green tea），分析其具備的營養成份及對健康的好處，並引述科學性的報導來支持這些論述，其閱讀重點如下：

① 大眾對綠茶的印象。
② 綠茶對身體的營養成分及益處。

🔵 文章閱讀 ••

Benefits of Green Tea

While green tea has long been valued in China and Japan for its medicinal **properties**, health-conscious people around the world are drinking green tea in record numbers. What's more, modern science is researching green tea's health benefits and **confirming** the ancient Chinese belief that "it is better to drink green tea than take medicine."

In addition to many essential acids and even fluoride, green tea has high levels of antioxidant properties that are known to prevent cancer. A cup of green tea **contains** vitamin B complex, vitamin E and more vitamin C than a whole orange. The American Medical Association claims that regular **consumption** of green tea can also cut cholesterol and lower the risk of stroke in men.

● 學習焦點 ┈┈┈┈┈┈┈┈┈┈┈┈┈┈┈┈┈┈┈┈┈┈┈┈┈┈┈┈┈┈┈┈┈┈┈┈┈

本文第一行點出綠茶與時俱增的重要性，引起大家對綠茶有那些益處的好奇心。

① 第一段以 "While green tea has long been valued in China and Japan for its medicinal properties…" 道出綠茶受到重視其來有自，接著說明科學家也證實綠茶的健康價值 "…it is better to drink green tea than take medicine."。

② 第二段進一步說明綠茶含有哪些營養成分：essential acids, fluoride, high levels of antioxidant properties, vitamin B complex, vitamin E, and Vitamin C 等。

③ 最後引述專業機構的聲明來引證喝綠茶的好處 "The American Medical Association claims that regular consumption of green tea can also cut cholesterol and lower the risk of stroke in men."，可以減低膽固醇，和降低中風的風險。

★ **Vocabulary**

＊ property：【名詞】特性

Green tea / has long been valued / in China and Japan / for its medicinal properties.

綠茶 / 長久以來被重視 / 在中國和日本 / 因為它的醫療特性

＊ confirm：【動詞】確認

用法：人 / 研究報告 ＋ confirm ＋ 想要證實的事物

Modern science / is researching green tea's health benefits / and confirming the ancient Chinese belief / that "it is better to drink green tea than take medicine."

現代科學 / 正在研究綠茶的健康益處 / 並確認古老中國信仰 / 喝綠茶比吃藥還好

＊ contain：【動詞】包含

用法：事物 ＋ contain ＋ 內容物 / 成分

A cup of green tea / contains / vitamin B complex, vitamin E, / and more Vitamin C than a whole orange.

一杯綠茶 / 包含 / 維他命 B 群、維他命 E / 和比一整顆柳橙還多的維他命 C

＊ consumption：【名詞】消耗，消費

The American Medical Association / claims / that regular consumption of green tea / can also / cut cholesterol.

美國醫學協會 / 聲稱 / 有規律的飲用綠茶 / 也可以 / 減少膽固醇

＊ 健康資訊常見名詞：

acid（酸）、fluoride（氟化物）、antioxidant（抗氧化物）、vitamin（維他命）、cholesterol（膽固醇）。

句型：主詞＋動詞（think, believe, claim）that ＋ S ＋ V

that 所引導的名詞子句（that ＋ S ＋ V）可以放在陳述性動詞（如 think, believe, state, claim）之後，用來陳述事實、表達意見、或釐清概念。

The American Medical Association claims <u>that regular consumption of green tea can also cut cholesterol and lower the risk of stroke in men.</u>

　　　　　　　　↑
　　表示美國醫學協會的觀點

動詞 claim（聲稱）後面接續的句子，是指美國醫學協會的觀點：有規律的飲用綠茶也可以減少膽固醇和降低人體中風的風險。

🌀 摘要與測驗重點提示 •••••••••••••••••••••••••••••••••••••

★ 閱讀要項

本篇文章須要注意的重點如下：

① 本文主題：Green tea
② 營養成分：essential acids, fluoride, antioxidant properties, vitamin
③ 對身體的好處：cutting cholesterol, lowering the risk of stroke

★ 常用字彙及句法

① 證明某種理論或說法：人 / 研究報告 ＋ confirm ＋ 想要證實的事物
② 說明某物所包含的內容：事物 ＋ contain ＋ 內容物 / 成份

本文章介紹綠茶受到重視的原因，它的健康好處受到醫學研究實證支持，所含營養成分能降低致病風險。

練習題

1. In what does modern medical science regard green tea?

a) Green tea lacks vitamins.

b) Research has proven the benefits of green tea.

c) Green tea has little medical value.

d) Drinking green tea can cure cancer.

2. How does green tea prevent cancer?

a) It contains many important vitamins.

b) It protects skin from the sun.

c) It has many antioxidants.

d) It contains essential acids and fluoride.

3. Which is true according to the article?

a) Green tea is only popular in East Asia.

b) Green tea provides every kind of nutrition.

c) Green tea can lower cholesterol.

d) People must drink green tea every day.

Benefits of Mushrooms

Mushrooms are good for your health. Researchers are looking at mushrooms for various medicinal purposes. In Japan, for example, scientists use the maitake mushroom to treat high blood pressure and lower cholesterol levels.

However, the curative effect of mushrooms shouldn't be overemphasized. Mushrooms alone can't make you healthier. In addition, you need a healthy lifestyle. Exercise, a balanced diet, and reducing stress can all lead to a healthy heart.

1. According to the article, what disease can be prevented by using mushrooms?

a) Headache

b) Depression

c) High blood pressure

d) Heart attack

2. In addition to mushrooms, what does the author suggest to stay healthy?

a) Eating a healthy diet

b) Fasting

c) Seeing a doctor

d) Drinking less wine

文章閱讀 翻譯與題解

文章翻譯

綠茶的保健妙用

　　綠茶長期以來在中國和日本因為具有療效而備受重視。如今全球飲用綠茶的養生人士越來越多，甚至連現代科學家也在研究綠茶對健康的益處，證實古代中國人「飲茶勝過吃藥」的說法。

　　綠茶除了包含許多人體必需的胺基酸和氟化物之外，綠茶本身含有大量被認為可以預防癌症的抗氧化物質。一杯綠茶含有維生素 B 群、維他命 E，其維他命 C 的含量甚至多於一整顆柳橙。美國醫療協會宣稱，固定攝取綠茶可同時減少膽固醇，並降低人們中風的風險。

題解

1. 解答：b) 研究已經證實綠茶的好處。

中譯：

現代醫學如何看待綠茶的功用？

a) 綠茶缺乏維他命。

b) 研究已經證實綠茶的好處。

c) 綠茶不太有療效。

d) 飲用綠茶可以治療癌症。

題解：第一段末尾的關鍵句提到 "…modern science is researching green tea's health benefits and confirming…"，句中的動詞 confirm「證實」和選項 b) 中的 prove「證明」呼應，故答案選 b) 最貼切。

Benefits of Green Tea　綠茶的保健妙用

健康環保篇

15

167

2. 解答：c）它含有許多抗氧化成分。

中譯：

綠茶如何預防癌症？

a）它富含許多重要的維生素。

b）它能保護皮膚免於陽光的傷害。

c）它含有許多抗氧化成分。

d）它含有人體必需的胺基酸和氟化物。

題解： 關鍵句為第二段第一句 "…green tea has high levels of antioxidant properties that are known to prevent cancer." 「綠茶因為含有大量的抗氧化物質所以能預防癌症」，故答案選 c）。

3. 解答：c）綠茶可以降低膽固醇。

中譯：

根據本文，下列何者為真？

a）綠茶只有在亞洲受歡迎。

b）綠茶提供各種營養成分。

c）綠茶可以降低膽固醇。

d）人人應該每天喝綠茶。

題解： 由文章最後一句可知，綠茶可有效降低膽固醇（cut cholesterol），故答案選 c）。

● 文章翻譯 ....

蕈菇好處多

　　蕈菇對健康有益。研究人員正積極研究將蕈菇作為不同醫療用途。例如在日本，科學家利用舞菇來治療高血壓及降低膽固醇。

　　然而，蕈菇的療效不應被過分強調。單憑蕈菇本身無法使人更健康。而還需要有健康的生活型態。搭配運動、均衡飲食以及減輕壓力，才能帶來健康的心臟。

● 題解 ....

1. 解答：c) 高血壓

中譯：

根據本文，蕈菇可以預防哪種疾病？

a) 頭痛

b) 憂鬱症

c) 高血壓

d) 心臟病

題解：由第一段末尾關鍵句 "...treat high blood pressure and lower cholesterol levels." 可知，蕈菇可以預防高血壓和降低膽固醇。

2. 解答：a）健康飲食

中譯：

除了蕈菇，本文作者還建議如何維持身體健康？

a）健康飲食

b）絕食

c）去看醫生

d）少喝酒

題解：本文第二段最後說明：除了食用蕈菇外，還必須配合均衡飲食（balanced diet）才是保持健康的關鍵，故答案選 a）最恰當。

16

Health Care Myth Busters
終結保健迷思

📖 閱讀重點 ••

本篇文章是討論膽囊問題的另類治療法（alternative remedy to treat gallbladder problems），其閱讀重點如下：

① 此療法的進行方式及宣稱的結果
② 此療法的不可靠處

🔵 文章閱讀 ••

Health Care Myth Busters

The "gallbladder flush" has become a fashionable remedy in **alternative** medicine. To do it, patients must drink four glasses of apple juice and eat five apples per day for five days. They must then fast briefly, take magnesium, and finally drink lots of lemon juice mixed with olive oil before bed. The next morning, they painlessly pass some green and brown stones.

A New Zealand hospital analyzed stones from a gallbladder flush and discovered they were made of fatty acids similar to those in olive oil, <u>with no cholesterol or bile salts detected</u>. This shows that they are in fact hardened olive oil.

Peter Duran, author of "The Truth about Gallbladder and Liver Flushes", says apple juice will never **reach** your gallstones because a muscle stops anything in your intestines from leaking back into your gallbladder. The so-called remedy may also **cause** side effects. This and similar recipes can make you experience nausea, diarrhea, vomiting, and abdominal pain. If you overdose on magnesium, it could even be fatal.

Before you try any alternative remedy to **treat** gallbladder problems, talk to your doctor.

● 學習焦點 ∙∙

時下有許多另類療法，排膽結石食療法是最近在網路上盛傳的方式之一。

① 第一段說明排膽結石食療法是如何進行的："drink four glasses of apple juice and eat five apples per day for five days"（連續五天、每天食用四杯蘋果汁和五顆蘋果），最後一天短暫禁食（fast briefly），服用鎂（magnesium）在睡前喝下大量摻了橄欖油的檸檬汁（lemon juice mixed with olive oil），隔天一早就可排出棕綠色的結石 "pass some green and brown stones"。

② 第二段以實驗分析這些綠棕色石狀物的成分："...they were made of fatty acids similar to those in olive oil."（他們是由相似於橄欖油的脂肪酸所組成），進而證明此療法的問題點。

172

③ 第三段再以專家的著作來佐證這類療法的疑點：蘋果汁無法接觸到結石，因為肌肉組織會阻擋腸道食物回流到膽囊 "...a muscle stops anything in your intestines from leaking back into your gallbladder"；同時指出此療法的副作用（side effects），包括噁心、腹瀉、嘔吐、腹痛（nausea, diarrhea, vomiting and abdominal pain），甚至會喪命 "...it could even be fatal."。

④ 最後建議在嘗試其他治療膽囊問題的方法時（any alternative remedy to treat gallbladder problems），別忘了先問醫生。

🌐 語言知識補充站 ⋯⋯⋯⋯⋯⋯⋯⋯⋯⋯⋯⋯⋯⋯⋯⋯⋯⋯⋯⋯⋯⋯

★ Vocabulary

＊ buster：【名詞】阻撓者；破壞者

通常是指具有破壞力的人或事物，例如本文主題 Health Care Myth Busters，就是指破壞一些人們口耳相傳的養生說法。

＊ alternative：【修飾詞】替代的；可供選擇的

The "gallbladder flush" / has become a fashionable remedy / in alternative medicine.

「膽囊沖洗淨化」法 / 已經成為一種時尚療法 / 在另類的醫藥領域中

＊ reach：【動詞】到達；接觸

Apple juice / will never reach your gallstones / because a muscle stops anything in your intestines / from leaking back into your gallbladder.

蘋果汁 / 不會接觸到膽結石 / 因為肌肉組織會阻擋任何腸道食物 / 回流進入膽囊

＊ cause：【動詞】引起

用法：原因 ＋ cause ＋ 結果

The so-called remedy / may / cause side effects.

所謂的治療法 / 可能 / 會引起副作用

Health Care Myth Busters 終結保健迷思 健康環保篇 16

＊ treat：【動詞】治療；處理。

用法：treat ＋ 疾病／問題

Before you try any alternative remedy / to treat gallbladder problems, / talk to your doctor.

在嘗試任何另類療法之前／去治療膽囊問題／跟你的醫生商量一下

＊健康資訊常見的字詞：

cholesterol（膽固醇）、gallbladder（膽囊）、intestine（腸子）、abdominal（腹部的）、nausea（噁心）、diarrhea（腹瀉）

★ Sentence Pattern

句型：S ＋ V, with ＋ N ＋ V-ed

with 所引導的片語通常表示一種情境或狀況，作為前面主要子句的補充說明。

A New Zealand hospital discovered stones from a gallbladder flush were made of fatty acids similar to those in olive oil, <u>with no cholesterol or bile salts detected.</u>

代表從膽囊沖洗法排出來的石頭並沒有偵測到膽固醇或膽汁鹽。

由於石頭是「被」偵測到的，因此用 V-ed（detected）。

摘要與測驗重點提示 ●●●

★ 閱讀要項

本篇文章須要注意的重點如下：

① 另類療法："gallbladder flush"（一種稱為膽囊沖洗淨化的療法）
② 爭議之處：Stones from a gallbladder flush were made of fatty acids similar to those in olive oil.（沖洗法排出的石頭成分近似橄欖油中的脂肪酸）

① 表示因果關係：原因 + cause + 結果
② 表示治療疾病：treat + 疾病 / 問題
③ 狀況補充說明：S + V, with + N + V-ed

★ 測驗重點

本文的重點資訊在於破解另類療法有效的傳言，並以醫生和專家意見為佐證。

練習題

1. What is a gallbladder flush?

a) An exercise

b) A hospital treatment

c) A non-conventional therapy

d) A drink of lemon juice and olive oil

2. What is the expert's opinion on the "gallbladder flush" ?

a) The recipe should be changed to be more effective.

b) Cholesterol was found in the stones from a gallbladder flush.

c) It was suggested that the patients undergo surgery afterward.

d) It could cause some digestive system disorders.

3. What can happen if you take too much magnesium?

a) It could be beneficial.

b) It will help you sleep.

c) It could kill you.

d) It will help you lose weight.

Health Care Myth Busters　終結保健迷思

16

健康環保篇

Food & Drink Medical Myth

Myth 1: Carrots can improve your eyesight

The origins of this go back to the Second World War. British intelligence services spread the rumor that their pilots ate lots of carrots and that's why they were so successful at destroying German targets. In reality, it was their use of radar which made them successful. The myth was so convincing that we still believe it today.

Myth 2: Eating spinach can make you stronger

The myth that spinach is full of iron emerged from a mistake in a report many years ago. In the report, spinach was noted to have 34 mg of iron (per half tin), while in reality it is only 3.4 mg. This typo led people to believe that spinach was full of iron. Because it was also low in price, it became very popular.

Myth 3: We need to drink at least eight glasses of water a day

A 60-year-old article by the USA National Academy of Sciences noted that adults should drink around 2.5 liters a day. In the same article they pointed out that this quantity is already in the food we eat. In other words we consume the water our body needs in the food we eat.

1. What is the purpose of this article?

a) To encourage people to eat more carrots

b) To dispel some misconceptions about food and drink

c) To point out what foods contain the most water

d) To introduce ways to eliminate errors in scientific writing

2. Why did the British government spread the rumor about carrots?

a) They didn't want to reveal their radar system.

b) They wanted to sell carrots to Germany.

c) They tried to create a medical myth.

d) They tried to mislead people about the nutrition contained in carrots.

3. For what other reason was spinach popular?

a) It was easy to cook.

b) It was cheap.

c) It was easy to find.

d) It was easy to grow.

文章閱讀 翻譯與題解

文章翻譯

終結保健迷思

「膽囊排石法」已經成為一種流行的另類民俗醫療方式。要達成這樣的治療，病患必須連續五天，每天飲用四杯蘋果汁，吃五顆蘋果。然後短暫禁食，服用鎂，最後，在睡前要喝下許多混了橄欖油的檸檬汁。隔天早晨，他們可以不感疼痛地排出綠色和棕色的結石。

一間紐西蘭的醫院分析了這些透過膽囊排石法排出的石子，發現它們是由近似於橄欖油中所含的脂肪酸組成，不含膽固醇或膽鹽。這顯示出那些排出來的結石事實上就是變硬的橄欖油而已。

《肝膽排石法的真相》一書的作者—彼得·杜蘭（Peter Duran）提到：「其實蘋果汁永遠到不了你的膽結石，因為腸子裡的肌肉會防止任何東西回流到你的膽囊內。這套所謂的治療法可能導致副作用。這個方法或其他相似的配方可能使你產生噁心、腹瀉、嘔吐和腹部的疼痛感。如果食用過量的鎂，也可能致命。」

在嘗試使用任何民俗療法治療膽囊問題前，最好先和你的醫生談談。

題解

1. 解答：c）一種非傳統性的療法。

中譯：

什麼是膽囊排石法？

a）一種運動

b）一種醫院的治療方式

c) 一種非傳統式的療法

d) 一種混合檸檬汁與橄欖油的飲料

題解：根據文章的描述可知，膽囊排石法，其實就是一種非經醫學實驗的民俗療法，故答案選 c)。

2. 解答：d) 可能導致一些消化系統失調的情況。

中譯：

專家對於「膽囊排石法」的見解為何？

a) 這個祕方應該調整成更有效的配方。

b) 利用膽囊排石法排出的結石中發現膽固醇。

c) 這意味著病患之後要接受手術治療。

d) 可能導致一些消化系統失調的情況。

題解：由文章末段的描述可知，專家認為膽囊排石法可能造成許多消化系統相關的後遺症，故答案選 d)。

3. 解答：c) 那可能致命。

中譯：

如果服用過量的鎂會發生什麼樣的情況？

a) 那會很有幫助。

b) 那會讓你入睡。

c) 那可能致命。

d) 會幫你減肥。

題解：由文章第三段最後一句話可知，服用過量的鎂可能會致命，故答案選 c)。

● 文章翻譯 ⋯⋯⋯⋯⋯⋯⋯⋯⋯⋯⋯⋯⋯⋯⋯⋯⋯⋯⋯⋯⋯⋯⋯⋯⋯⋯

食物和飲料的療效迷思

迷思一：吃胡蘿蔔可以增進視力

這個迷思源自第二次世界大戰。英國的情報單位散佈謠言說他們的飛行員因為吃了許多胡蘿蔔，所以可以準確地摧毀德軍的標的。事實上，是因為有雷達的幫忙，他們才能成功達陣。這個迷思很有說服力，以致於我們今天還深信不疑。

迷思二：吃菠菜可以讓人變得更強壯

菠菜富含鐵質的迷思是來自一則多年前錯誤的報導。報導中註明菠菜含有 34 毫克的鐵，但事實上只含有 3.4 毫克。打字排版的錯誤導致人們誤以為菠菜富含鐵質。也因為它的價格低廉，所以還是很受歡迎。

迷思三：每人一天至少要喝八杯水

一篇六十年前美國國家研究院發表的文章指出一位成人一天至少要飲用約 2.5 公升的水，同篇文章中還提出，這樣的喝水量已經包含在我們每天攝取的食物中。換句話說我們從吃下去的食物中，已經吸收了身體所需的水分。

1. 解答：b) 破除一些關於飲食的錯誤觀念。

中譯：

本篇文章的主旨為何？

a) 鼓勵人們多吃胡蘿蔔

b) 破除一些關於飲食的錯誤觀念

c) 指出哪些食物含有最多水分

d) 介紹去除科學文獻謬誤的方法

題解：本文指出關於飲食方面的誤解和迷思，故答案選 b) 最貼切。

2. 解答：a) 他們不想洩漏他們採用雷達系統。

中譯：

為何英國政府要散播關於胡蘿蔔的謠言？

a) 他們不想洩漏他們採用雷達系統。

b) 他們想把胡蘿蔔賣到德國。

c) 他們試圖製造醫療迷思。

d) 他們試圖誤導人們對胡蘿蔔所含養分的認識。

題解：由文章中提到的第一個迷思可知，會有如此錯誤的謠傳，是因為英國想掩蓋使用雷達偵測的事實，故答案選 a)。

3. 解答：b) 它很便宜。

中譯：

有哪些其他原因使菠菜受歡迎？

a) 它易於烹調。

b) 它很便宜。

c) 它很容易找到。

d) 它很好種植。

題解：由文章中第二項迷思的最後一句可知，菠菜很便宜所以即使科學報告打錯營養成分，它還是很受歡迎，故答案選 b)。

科普知識篇

17

The Origin of Bungee Jumping
高空彈跳的由來

17

閱讀重點

高空彈跳屬於驚險刺激的極限運動（extreme sport），不過它的起源（origin）
卻很有趣，本文以此為主題，其閱讀重點如下：

① 高空彈跳的起源與演變。
② 高空彈跳可能有的風險

文章閱讀

The Origin of Bungee Jumping

The origin of bungee jumping can be **traced** back to a documentary
of the "land divers" of Pentecost Island in Vanuatu about young men
who jumped from tall wooden platforms <u>with vines tied to their ankles</u>
as a test of courage.

The first modern bungee jump was made on April 1979 from the
250ft Clifton Suspension Bridge in Bristol, England, but the jumpers

were **arrested** shortly after. However, followers in the US made jumps from the Golden Gate and Royal Gorge bridges, which was **broadcast** on the American TV program "That's Incredible" and helped spread the concept worldwide.

Although this activity is very **attractive** to young people, there is a high risk of getting injured during a jump. The factors contributing to the **injuries** include age, equipment, experience, location, weight, and the psychological status of the jumper.

學習焦點 ••

本文分三段：

① 第一段 "The origin of bungee jumping can be traced back to a documentary of the 'land divers' of Pentecost Island in Vanuatu…" 點出文章主旨是敘述高空彈跳的源起－來自南太平洋的小島上一種從高處躍下的儀式。

② 第二段敘述高空彈跳的演變，包括第一個現代版的彈跳舉動是在英國 "The first modern bungee jump was made on April 1979 from the 250ft Clifton Suspension Bridge in Bristol, England…"，不過彈跳者事後遭到逮捕。

③ 彈跳真正成為全球風氣則是拜美國電視節目轉播金門大橋等地的彈跳活動："followers in the US made jumps from the Golden Gate and Royal Gorge bridges, which was broadcast on the American TV program 'That's Incredible' and helped spread the concept worldwide."。

④ 第三段說明高空彈跳的可能風險，包括年齡、設備、經驗、地點、體重和心理狀態 "The factors contributing to the injuries include age, equipment, experience, location, weight and the psychological status of the jumper."。

17

★ **Vocabulary**

* trace：【動詞】追溯
用法：人 / 事 / 物 + be traced to + 起源的事物或時間點
The origin of bungee jumping / can be traced back to / a documentary / of the "land divers" / of Pentecost Island in Vanuatu.
高空彈跳的起源 / 可以被追溯至 / 一部紀錄片 / 有關高處躍下的人 / 在萬那杜的聖靈島

* arrest：【動詞】逮捕
用法：人 + be arrested
The jumpers / were arrested / after they made the first modern bungee jump / in Bristol, England / on April 1979.
高空彈跳者 / 被逮捕 / 在他們完成第一個現代高空彈跳之後 / 在英國布里斯托 / 於 1979 年四月間

* broadcast：【動詞】廣播；播送
Followers in the US / made jumps from the Golden Gate and Royal Gorge bridges, / which was broadcast on a TV program / and helped spread the concept worldwide.
美國的追隨者 / 從金門大橋和皇家峽谷大橋完成彈跳 / 在電視節目上轉播 / 協助散播此概念到全世界

* attractive：【修飾語】吸引人的
用法：be attractive to + 人
Although / this activity / is very attractive to young people, / there is a high risk of getting injured / during a jump.
雖然 / 這活動 / 非常吸引年輕人 / 仍有高度的受傷風險 / 在彈跳時

＊ injury：【名詞】傷害

The factors / contributing to the injuries / include age, equipment, experience, location, weight / and the psychological status of the jumper.
某些因素 / 造成傷害 / 包括年齡、設備、經驗、地點、體重 / 和彈跳者的心理狀態

★ Sentence Pattern

以片語開頭的句型：S ＋ V, with ＋ N ＋ V-ed ...,

with 所帶出來的介係詞片語是傳達一種情境或條件。

The origin of bungee jumping can be traced back to a documentary of the "land divers" of Pentecost Island in Vanuatu about young men who jumped from tall wooden platforms with vines tied to their ankles as a test of courage.

with 引導的片語代表某種情境，表示這些人是在腳踝綁著籐條的狀況下，從高聳的平台跳下來，請注意 with 後面接的名詞 vines，因為藤條是「被綁」在腳踝上，所以用 V-ed 的形式（tied）。

🌀 摘要與測驗重點提示 ••

★ 閱讀要項

本篇文章須要注意的重點如下：

① 文章主題：bungee jump
② 起源：a documentary of the "land divers" of Pentecost Island in Vanuatu
③ 發展：the jumpers in England and the followers in the US
④ 風險因素：age, equipment, experience, location, weight and the
　　　　　　 psychological status of the jumper

① 追溯起源：人／事／物 + be traced to + 起源的事物或時間點
② 吸引某人：be attractive to + 人

★ 測驗重點

本文章的重點資訊是高空彈跳的起源，以及該活動如何在全世界蔚為風氣，並附帶叮嚀高空彈跳可能造成的危險。

練習題

1. What is the objective of the land diving ceremony in Vanuatu?

a) To entertain guests from all over the world

b) To celebrate the founding of a country

c) To be a test of the jumpers' courage

d) To make a documentary

2. What happened after a bungee jump was made on Clifton Suspension Bridge?

a) The jumpers were arrested.

b) The jumpers were sent to hospital.

c) The incident was broadcast on a TV program.

d) The bridge was destroyed.

3. Which is NOT the cause of bungee jumping injuries?

a) Lack of equipment

b) Jumper's age

c) Jumper's mental status

d) Jumper's sex

The Origin of Football

The origin of football has been debated for years. About 2,500 years ago in China there was a similar game called "Cuju", which, according to the International Football Association, was the origin of football as a sport. In China, "cu" means "kick" and "ju" is a type of leather ball filled with feathers.

According to historical records, cuju was a very popular and widespread game in China's Spring and Autumn Period 770BC~476BC. The game also influenced China's neighbor, Japan. The sport was introduced into Japan 1,400 years ago by returning Japanese emissaries and students who had learned it in China.

1. What is the article mainly about?

a) The introduction of the football sport into China

b) The making of a football

c) The popularity of the football game in China

d) The beginning of a popular sport

2. According to the article, what was the first "football" made of?

a) Paper

b) Leather

c) Plastic

d) Rubber

3. Who introduced the football sport into Japan?

a) Chinese students

b) Chinese envoys

c) Japanese delegates

d) A Japanese empress

高空彈跳的由來

　　高空彈跳的起源可以追溯自萬那杜聖靈島上一部有關「從高處躍下的人」的紀錄片。那是該島上一群年輕人，在腳踝綑綁藤索後，從高聳的木製平台跳下，以此測試個人的勇氣。

　　首次現代版的高空彈跳，發生於 1979 年 4 月，彈跳者從英格蘭布里斯托一座 250 英尺高的克利夫敦吊橋上一躍而下，但他們隨後就被逮捕了。然而在美國，高空彈跳的愛好者們，從金門大橋及皇家峽谷大橋高空彈跳的畫面，在美國的電視節目「信不信由你！」播出後，助長此活動概念傳遍全球。

　　雖然這項活動對年輕人而言極具吸引力，但跳躍的過程仍有不慎受傷的高風險。造成傷害的因素包含跳躍者之年齡、配備、經驗、地點、體重及當時的心理狀態。

● 題解

1. 解答：c）為了測試跳躍者的勇氣

中譯：

萬那杜的「從高處躍下」的儀式目的為何？

a）為了娛樂來自全球的賓客

b）為了慶祝建國大典

c）為了測試跳躍者的勇氣

d）為了製作紀錄片

題解：本題關鍵句為第一段最後一句，可知該儀式的目的在藉由高空跳躍測試一個人是否夠勇敢，故答案選 c)。

2. 解答：a) 跳躍者們被逮捕了。

中譯：

在克利夫敦吊橋進行高空彈跳後，發生了什麼事？

a) 跳躍者們被逮捕了。

b) 跳躍者們被送去醫院。

c) 這個活動在電視節目播出了。

d) 那座吊橋被毀了。

題解：由文章第二段內容可知，跳躍者們就被逮捕了，故答案選 a)。

3. 解答：d) 彈跳者的性別

中譯：

下列哪一項不是導致高空彈跳後受傷的原因？

a) 缺乏裝備

b) 彈跳者的年齡

c) 彈跳者的心理狀態

d) 彈跳者的性別

題解：由文章最後一段可知，選項 d) 不在文章所列的原因之中，故選 d)。

延伸閱讀 翻譯與題解

● 文章翻譯 ....

足球的由來

　　足球的由來多年來一直爭辯不休。兩千五百年前的中國，流傳著一項與足球相似的遊戲叫作「蹴鞠」，被國際足球聯盟認定為足球這項運動的起源。中文裡「蹴」的意思就是踢，而「鞠」則指一種以羽毛填充的皮球。

　　根據歷史資料顯示，蹴鞠是一項在中國春秋時代（西元前 770 年～西元前 476 年間）非常受歡迎且普遍的遊戲。這項遊戲也傳播到中國的鄰國—日本。此運動在一千四百年前被日本派至中國的特使及留學生習得後，他們返國時，便引進日本。

● 題解 ....

1. 解答：d）一項熱門運動的起源

中譯：

這篇文章的主旨是關於？

a）足球運動如何被引進中國

b）足球的製作過程

c）足球遊戲在中國受歡迎的程度

d）一項熱門運動的起源

題解：由文章的標題及第一段中之內容可推知，答案選 d）最恰當。

The Origin of Bungee Jumping　高空彈跳的由來 科普知識篇

17

2. 解答：b) 皮革

中譯：

根據本文，第一顆「足球」是由什麼材料製成的？

a) 紙張

b) 皮革

c) 塑膠

d) 橡膠

題解：由第一段末尾解釋「蹴鞠」的意思可知，最早的足球是由皮革製成，故答案選 b)。

3. 解答：c) 日本的使節團

中譯：

是誰將足球運動介紹到日本的呢？

a) 中國學生

b) 中國的外交使節

c) 日本的使節團

d) 一位日本女天皇

題解：由文章第二段末尾可知，足球是透過日本派到中國的特使及留學生介紹回日本的。

18

UVB and UVA Protection
防曬知多少：紫外線 A 光和 B 光

18

閱讀重點 ···

許多人在購買或使用商品時，對於產品標籤（label）裡的一些專業術語（technical terms），常會感到困惑；本文以防曬產品標示中常看到的 UVB 和 UVA 為例，其閱讀重點如下：

① UVB 和 UVA 代表的意義。
② 如何預防皮膚癌。

文章閱讀 ···

UVB and UVA Protection

　　Recent research shows that people who buy **sunscreen** products aren't sure about the technical terms on their labels.

　　UVA (ultraviolet-A): UVA sun rays refer to long-wave solar rays which **remain** the same strength no matter how close or how far away the sun is from the earth. UVA penetrates the skin more deeply and is

18

considered the main cause behind wrinkling and aging.

    UVB (ultraviolet-B): UVB sun rays refer to short-wave solar rays which are stronger than UVA in producing **sunburn**. These rays are considered the main cause of **melanoma**.

    To **prevent** skin cancer, a thorough protection is needed, which includes the use of sunscreen products along with sun-protective clothing, sunglasses, and sun avoidance from 10 A.M. to 4 P.M.

● 學習焦點 ••

文分四段：

① 第一段以研究調查的結果（Recent research shows that...）增加文章的客觀性，說明人們在購買防曬產品時並不了解標籤裡的專門術語："...people who buy sunscreen products aren't sure about the technical terms on their labels."。

② 第二段主要說明UVA（ultraviolet-A）的意義及對皮膚的傷害："UVA sun rays refer to long-wave solar rays..."（ UVA是一種光波長的紫外線），它也是皺紋和老化的主要因素 "...the main cause behind wrinkling and aging."。

③ 第三段說明UVB（ultraviolet-B）的意義及對皮膚的傷害：UVB指的是波光短的紫外線 "UVB sun rays refer to short-wave solar rays."，被視為皮膚黑色腫瘤的主要原因 "These rays are considered the main cause of melanoma."。

④ 第四段談要如何預防皮膚癌："...includes the use of sunscreen products along with sun-protective clothing, sunglasses, and sun avoidance from 10 A.M. to 4 P.M." 包括防曬乳產品的使用，再搭配防曬衣物、太陽眼鏡、和早上十點到下午四點期間避免日曬。

★ **Vocabulary**

✳ sunscreen：【名詞】防曬劑

Recent research / shows / that people aren't sure about / the technical terms / on the labels of sunscreen products.

最近研究 / 顯示 / 人們不確定 / 專業術語 / 在防曬產品標籤上

✳ remain：【動詞】維持

用法：人 / 物 ＋ remain ＋ 表示「狀態」的字詞

UVA sun rays / remain the same strength / no matter how close or how far away / the sun is from the earth.

UVA 太陽光線 / 維持相同強度 / 不論多近或是多遠 / 太陽距離地球

✳ consider：【動詞】考慮；認為

用法：人 / 物 ＋ be considered ＋ 被視為的事物

UVA / penetrates / the skin more deeply / and is considered / the main cause behind wrinkling and aging.

UVA / 穿透 / 更深入肌膚 / 且被認為是 / 皺紋和老化的主要原因

✳ sunburn：【名詞】曬傷；曬黑

UVB sun rays / refer to / short-wave solar rays / which are stronger than UVA / in producing sunburn.

UVB 太陽光線 / 指的是 / 短波的太陽光線 / 比 UVA 還要強烈 / 造成曬傷

✳ melanoma：【名詞】皮膚黑色素瘤

These rays / are considered / the main cause of melanoma.

這些光線 / 被認為是 / 黑色素瘤的主要原因

18

＊ prevent：【動詞】預防；阻止

用法：人 / 物 ＋ prevent ＋ 想要預防發生的事情

To prevent skin cancer, / a thorough protection / is needed / which includes the use of sunscreen products / along with sun-protective clothing, sunglasses, / and sun avoidance from 10 A.M. to 4 P.M.

為了預防皮膚癌 / 徹底的防護 / 是需要的 / 包括防曬產品的使用 / 配合防曬衣物、太陽眼鏡 / 和早上十點到下午四點期間避免日曬

★ Sentence Pattern

句型：$S_1 + V_1 + N + （which + S_2 + V_2）$

which 所引導的子句主要是說明前面的事物，傳達特定資訊及狀況給讀者。

UVB sun rays refer to short-wave solar rays which are stronger than UVA in producing sunburn.

which 指前面的 solar rays，表示這種光線比 UVA 更容易造成皮膚曬傷。

摘要與測驗重點提示 ●●●●●●●●●●●●●●●●●●●●●●●●●●●●●●●●●●●●

★ 閱讀要項

本篇文章須要注意的重點如下：

① 解釋名詞：UVA sun rays refer to long-wave solar rays.
　　　　　　 UVB sun rays refer to short-wave solar rays.
② 對人體的影響：UVA → the main cause behind wrinkling and aging.
　　　　　　　　 UVB → the main cause of melanoma
③ 防範措施：sunscreen products, sun-protective clothing, sunglasses, and sun avoidance from 10 A.M. to 4 P.M.

與防曬有關字彙：UVA, UVB, sunscreen, sunburn, aging, wrinkling, skin cancer, melanoma

★ 測驗重點

本文重點資訊為認識 UVB 和 UVA，以及對健康的影響。

練習題

1. What is the purpose of the article?

a) To tell people how to choose sunscreen products

b) To provide information about skin cancer treatment

c) To explain some technical terms

d) To describe signs of melanoma

2. What is true about ultraviolet rays?

a) UVA and UVB have the same wavelengths.

b) UVB sun rays are considered the main cause of melanoma.

c) UVB sun rays are the main cause of skin aging.

d) The wavelength of UVA rays will vary with the distance between the sun and the earth.

3. When are the peak hours for sun rays?

a) 9 A.M. to 2 P.M.

b) 10 P.M. to 4 A.M.

c) 10 A.M. to 4 P.M.

d) 10 A.M. to 5 P.M.

UVB and UVA Protection　防曬知多少：紫外線 A 光和 B 光　科普知識篇

18

Radiation Scare from Mobile Phones

Recently there is more evidence of health effects of mobile phone radiation on human health ranging from blood pressure to brain tumors. A Germany study showed that the blood pressure rose by 5-10 mm Hg whenever the mobile phones were attached to the heads of volunteers. Other studies in animals suggest that electromagnetic radiation from mobiles may cause brain tumors, cancer, anxiety, memory loss, and serious birth defects.

However, the greatest risk to a mobile phone user is from an accident while talking to someone by mobile phone when driving. This risk is likely to be many thousands of times greater than the danger from radiation.

1. What did the study results show in the article?

a) Blood pressure increased when using a mobile phone.

b) Brain tumors grew bigger when using a mobile phone.

c) Car drivers could concentrate when using a mobile phone.

d) Pregnant women feel depressed when using a mobile phone.

2. According to the article, which is the most dangerous effect of using mobile phones?

a) Brain tumor

b) Anxiety

c) Car accidents

d) Memory loss

UVB and UVA Protection　防曬知多少：紫外線Ａ光和Ｂ光　科普知識篇

18

文章閱讀 翻譯與題解

文章翻譯

防曬知多少：紫外線Ａ光和Ｂ光

近來的研究結果顯示，購買防曬商品的消費者其實並不清楚產品標籤上的專業術語。

UVA（紫外線-Ａ光）：

陽光紫外線Ａ光指的是長波的太陽光線，不論地球距離太陽多近或多遠，它都會維持固定的強度。紫外線Ａ光會穿透至皮膚深層，且被認為是造成皺紋和老化的背後主因。

UVB（紫外線-Ｂ光）：

陽光紫外線Ｂ光指的是短波長的太陽光線，較紫外線Ａ光來得強烈且會造成曬紅或曬傷的狀況。這些光線被認為是引發皮膚黑色素瘤的主要成因。

為避免得到皮膚癌，做好徹底地防護是必須的，包括使用防曬產品以及穿戴防曬的衣物、太陽眼鏡，並避免在上午十點到下午四點間曝曬於陽光下。

題解

1. 解答：c）解釋一些專業術語

中譯：

本文的主旨為何？

a）教導人們如何選擇防曬產品

b）提供關於治療皮膚癌的資訊

c）解釋一些專業術語

d）描述黑色素瘤產生的症狀

題解：本文第一段即說明人們多半對防曬商品中的專業術語並不瞭解，內文旨在說明專業術語代表的意思，故答案選 c）。

2. 解答：b）紫外線 B 光被認為是引發皮膚黑色素瘤的主因。

中譯：

下列關於紫外線的描述何者正確？

a）UVA（紫外線 A 光）和 UVB（紫外線 B 光）有相同的波長。

b）紫外線 B 光被認為是引發皮膚黑色素瘤的主因。

c）紫外線 B 光是造成皮膚老化的主因。

d）紫外線 A 光的波長會隨地球和太陽的距離而改變。

題解：由文章第三段說明紫外線 B 光的意義可知，選項 b）是正確的。

3. 解答：c）上午十點到下午四點

中譯：

什麼時候的陽光紫外線最強？

a）上午九點到下午兩點

b）下午十點到上午四點

c）上午十點到下午四點

d）上午十點到下午五點

題解：由文章最後一句關鍵句可知，上午十點到下午四點是紫外線最強的時候，故答案選 c）最合適。

18

● 文章翻譯 ⋯⋯⋯⋯⋯⋯⋯⋯⋯⋯⋯⋯⋯⋯⋯⋯⋯⋯⋯⋯⋯⋯⋯⋯⋯⋯⋯

恐怖的行動電話電磁波

　　近來有越來越多證據顯示手機電磁波對人體健康產生的影響，反映在血壓改變到腦瘤等層面。一項德國的研究顯示，當手機貼附在受試者腦部附近時，他的血壓會上升 5-10 毫米汞柱。其他在動物身上進行的研究亦指出，手機所發射的電磁波可能造成腦瘤、癌症、焦慮、喪失記憶和嚴重畸胎等情形。

　　然而，對於手機使用者來說，最大的風險來自邊開車邊講手機導致的意外事故。這項風險可能遠比電磁波帶來的危害多出成千上萬倍。

1. 解答：a) 使用手機時血壓會升高。

中譯：

本文中引用的研究結果顯示了什麼情況？

a) 使用手機時血壓會升高。

b) 使用手機時腦瘤會長更大。

c) 汽車駕駛講手機時能專心開車。

d) 孕婦使用手機時會感到心情沮喪。

題解：由文章內容提到的研究結果可推知，答案選 a) 最恰當。

2. 解答：c) 車禍

中譯：

根據本文，下列哪項是使用手機時會造成的最嚴重後果？

a) 腦瘤

b) 焦慮

c) 車禍

d) 喪失記憶

題解：由文章第二段可知，邊講手機邊開車最常造成慘重的結果，故答案選 c)。

19

The Happiest Age
最快樂的年齡

⌢19⌣

閱讀重點 ···

本篇文章指出人生最快樂的時期並非青少年時，而是四十六歲以後，其閱讀重點如下：

① 快樂滿足感隨著年齡的增減變化
② 造成各年齡層快樂感受差異的原因

文章閱讀 ···

The Happiest Age

　　Remember those carefree school days? They are often considered the happiest time in a person's life. But scientists have found out: it's just not true. We are most **content** when we reach the ripe age of 74.

　　According to the results of a long-term British survey, happiness **decreases** when you become a teenager. That may be no big surprise. However, we continue to feel less and less content <u>until</u> we turn 40.

From here, happiness levels stay about the same for a few years. Around the age of 46, our feelings of contentedness slowly rise again and reach a climax 30 years later.

What explanations can researchers offer for these findings? It is possible that as we get older, we become more grateful for what we have. We may also become better at dealing with negative emotions. While in our twenties and thirties, on the other hand, we face the pressures of pursuing a career and bringing up a family.

Dr Carlo Strenger, of Israel's Tel Aviv University, who was a member of the research team, said the key point was to make good use of what you learn about yourself in the first half of your life to make the second half more fulfilling.

"Most people can anticipate a second life, if not a second career."

學習焦點

你快樂嗎?英國一項針對不同年齡層的人對快樂感受的調查,似乎印證了「知足常樂」的道理。

① 第一段先以一項研究報告的結果 "We are most content when we reach the ripe age of 74."(我們最滿足的時候是達到七十四歲時),來推翻一般人以為學校生活時期才是最快樂的看法。

② 第二段說明滿足感是如何隨著年齡而變化:當人們進入青少年時期,快樂感開始下降,直到四十歲之前,會覺得越來越不滿足(feel less and less content),四十到四十六歲時,快樂的程度是持平沒有變化的,四十六歲之後才會越來越知足 "our feelings of contentedness slowly rise again."。

19

③ 第三段分析這份研究的意義：當人們年紀大時會感恩自己所擁有的一切（become more grateful for what we have），也較善於處理負面情緒（dealing with negative emotions），自然感到知足又快樂。

④ 第四段提出專家意見：善用你在前半段生命中學到有關自己的知識，"...make good use of what you learn about yourself in the first half of your life."，使第二段人生更加充實 "...make the second half more fulfilling."。

⑤ 最後以一句話作結論：就算沒有第二職涯的話，大多數人仍可預期人生的第二春："Most people can anticipate a second life, if not a second career."。

● 語言知識補充站 ••

★ Vocabulary

＊ content：【修飾語】滿足的；滿意的
We / are most content / when we / reach the ripe age of 74
我們 / 是最滿足的 / 當我們 / 到達七十四歲的成熟年齡

＊ decrease：【動詞】減少；降低
According to / the results of a long-term British survey, / happiness decreases / when you / become a teenager.
根據 / 英國的長期調查結果 / 快樂感降低 / 當你 / 變成青少年時

＊ grateful：【修飾語】感激的；感恩的
用法：人 ＋ become ＋ grateful ＋ for ＋ 事物
It is possible that / as we get older, / we become more grateful / for what we have.
這是有可能的 / 當我們變老時 / 我們變得更感恩 / 對我們所擁有的

* pressure：【名詞】壓力

While in our twenties and thirties, / we face the pressures / of pursuing a career / and bringing up a family.

在我們二、三十歲的時候 / 我們面對壓力 / 追求事業 / 和養家活口

* anticipate：【動詞】預期；預先作準備

Most people can anticipate / a second life, / if not a second career.

大多數的人可以預期 / 人生第二春 / 如果沒有第二個職涯

★ **Sentence Pattern**

句型：$S_1 + V_1 + $ until $ + S_2 + V_2$（特定時間點）

本句型是表示某一個動作（V1）一直持續到 until 後面敘述的時間點為止。

We continue to feel less and less content <u>until we turn 40</u>.

表示持續覺得越來越不滿足（continue to feel less and less content），這個動作一直到 until 後面帶出的時間點（turn 40）進入四十歲時為止。

摘要與測驗重點提示 ●●●●●●●●●●●●●●●●●●●●●●●●●●●

★ 閱讀要項

本篇文章須要注意的重點如下：

① 敘述主題：the happiest time in a person's life
② 原因分析：As we get older, we become more grateful for what we have, and better at dealing with negative emotions.

19

① 對某事覺得感激：人 + become + grateful + for + 事情
② 表示某個動作持續到特定的時間點：

S$_1$ + V$_1$ + until + S$_2$ + V$_2$（特定時間點）

★ 測驗重點

本文的重點資訊在於人生不同年齡階段的內心滿足程度變化，並解釋其原因。

練習題

1. What is the purpose of this article?

a) To explain the relationship between money and happiness

b) To emphasize the importance of finding a good job

c) To reveal the secrets behind having a happy life

d) To show the results of a survey

2. According to the article, what is the most unhappy age?

a) The teen years

b) The twenties

c) Middle age

d) Old age

3. What chart will best represent the change of happiness level described in the article?

a) A U-shaped curve

b) An S-shaped curve

c) A W-shaped curve

d) An M-shaped curve

The Hemline Index

What are the signs of a bad economy? High unemployment? Low birth rate? More crime? Well, all of that, and long skirts. In 1926 professor George Taylor from the University of Pennsylvania came up with the hemline index. The theory suggests that hemlines on women's dresses rise along with stock prices: the higher the stock prices, the shorter the dress. It is a strange theory, but in fact, recent research shows it is valid.

1920s – During the roaring '20s, stocks soared. Fashion became much more daring, and women wore very short skirts.

1930s – Along comes the Great Depression, and skirts get longer again.

1940s and 1950s – The economy is recovering from World War II. Things are not great, but the economy is certainly looking up. Women typically wear skirts that go to their knees.

1960s – Now is the time of the mini skirt, invented in 1965. The 1960s were also a time of huge economic growth.

1970s – The stock market plunges in the mid '70s, sending the hemline almost down to the ankles.

1980s – The economy prospers, and women start to wear shorter skirts. The '80s are also the age of the so-called power suit, a stiff office suit with wide shoulder pads.

1990s – People finally feel extremely confident about the economy, and miniskirts make their comeback.

2000s – 2008 saw the start of the biggest economic crisis since the Great Depression. Fashion experts have observed that longer and bohemian style skirts have started to become fashionable once again.

Want to know how the economy is doing? Take a look at what the women around you are wearing.

練習題

1. What is the purpose of this article?

a) To analyze the factors that affect stock prices

b) To explain why some women prefer short skirts

c) To illustrate the skirt length theory with historical data

d) To interpret the evolution of fashion in America

2. According to this article, what statement is true?

a) Fashion magazines may contain signs about economic growth.

b) Professor Taylor developed this theory during the Great Depression.

c) The hemline theory was based on data collected in the 1960s.

d) As the economy gets better, women wear longer skirts.

文章閱讀 翻譯與題解

● 文章翻譯 ‧‧

最快樂的年齡

還記得那段無憂無慮的學生生涯嗎？這段時光通常被認為是一個人一生中最快樂的日子。但科學家發現：這並不是事實。當人們年屆 74 歲之時，才是人生中最感知足的年紀。

根據一項長期在英國進行的調查結果顯示，當人們進入青少年時期，快樂的感覺就開始下降。這也許不令人意外。然而，人們直到四十歲，都會持續感覺越來越不滿足。年屆四十以後，快樂的程度大致會維持在同樣的水準幾年。大約到了 46 歲，人們對人生的滿足感會再度緩升一些，並在往後的三十年達到高峰。

研究人員可以為這些發現提供那些解釋呢？可能性之一是，當我們年齡漸長，人們越會對自己所擁有的一切懷有感恩之情。也可能是我們變得更善於處理負面情緒。從另一方面來看，當人們在二十幾歲和三十幾歲的時候，都正面臨追求事業與撫養家庭的壓力。

曾是該研究團隊成員之一的以色列台拉維夫大學教授─卡羅‧史創格說道：「關鍵在於要善用你前半生發掘到的自我潛能，充分發揮這些潛能，才能讓自己的下半生更豐富充實。」

「就算沒有事業第二春，多數人仍可以期望人生的第二春。」

1. 解答：d) 顯示一項研究的結果

中譯：

這篇文章的主旨為何？

a) 說明金錢和快樂之間的關係

b) 強調找到一份好工作的重要性

c) 透露擁有快樂人生背後的祕辛

d) 顯示一項研究的結果

題解：由文章第二段開頭即內文可知，本文主要在說明一項研究的結果，故答案選 d)。

2. 解答：c) 中年時

中譯：

根據本文，最不快樂的年齡是指幾歲？

a) 十幾歲的時候

b) 二十幾歲時

c) 中年時

d) 老年時

題解：由文章第三段末尾可知，當人們年屆二十到三十幾歲間，面臨事業和家庭雙重壓力下，是最容易不快樂的一段時光，故答案選 c)。

3. 解答：a) U 形曲線圖

中譯：

哪一種圖表最能表現本文所描述快樂程度改變的狀況？

a) U 形曲線圖

b) S 形曲線圖

c) W 形曲線圖

d) M 形曲線圖

題解：由文章的描述可知，人的滿足感會在四十歲之前會逐漸下降，之後才會緩升，故 U 形曲線最能表現這樣的變化趨勢，答案選 a) 最合適。

● 文章翻譯 ....

裙襬指數

　　經濟下滑的指標是什麼呢？是高失業率？低生育率？不斷攀升的犯罪率問題嗎？沒錯，以上皆是，還有一項─長裙因素。1926 年時，賓夕法尼亞大學教授喬治‧泰勒想出了這樣一個裙襬指數。這項指數假設女性的裙襬長度會隨著股價變動：當股價愈高，女性的裙擺愈短。這是個奇怪的理論，但事實上，最近研究顯示這項理論是成立的。

1920 年代─活躍的二〇年代股價飛漲。流行趨勢變得更大膽，女生穿著非常短的短裙。

1930 年代─緊接而來的大蕭條，裙子再度變長了。

1940 和 1950 年代─經濟從二次大戰後復甦。一切當然不完美，但經濟狀況逐漸看俏。此時婦女一般穿著及膝裙。

1960 年代─ 1965 年，迷你裙被發明後，這正是迷你裙的時代！同時也是經濟大成長的時期。

1970 年代─股票市場在七〇年代中期跌入谷底，讓裙襬幾乎長到接近腳踝。

1980 年代─經濟繁榮了起來，女性再度開始穿起較短的裙子。八〇年代同時也是所謂威力西裝的時代，就是指穿著一套有寬厚墊肩的硬挺正式西裝。

1990 年代─人們終於對經濟充滿信心，也讓迷你裙再度出現。

2000 年代─ 2008 年見證了自經濟大蕭條以來，所面臨最大的經濟危機。時尚專家觀察、預測出：裙襬長度較長且帶有波西米亞風的裙子，將會再度開始成為流行款式。

　　想知道目前的經濟狀況嗎？看看你身邊的女性穿什麼吧！

題解 ....

1. 解答：c）以歷史資料說明裙襬長度理論

中譯：

本文的主旨為何？

a）分析影響股價的因素

b）解釋為何有些婦女偏好穿短裙

c）以歷史資料說明裙襬長度理論

d）解釋美國時尚趨勢的演進史

題解：由本文的標題及內文描述可推知，全文主要說明裙襬理論，和歷史資料相互印證，故答案選 c）。

2. 解答：a）流行雜誌可能包含有關經濟成長的徵兆。

中譯：

根據本文描述，下列何者敘述正確？

a）流行雜誌可能包含有關經濟成長的徵兆。

b）泰勒教授在經濟大蕭條時期建立了這個理論。

c）裙襬理論是基於 1960 年代蒐集的資料建立的。

d）當經濟狀況好轉時，女性會穿著較長的裙子。

題解：本文主要是透過觀察流行趨勢與經濟情況的關係，故答案選 a）最合理。

20

Doomsday Prophecy of 2012
2012 年末日預言

20

閱讀重點

本篇文章是討論今年大家最關心的話題之一：2012 年末日預言（Doomsday Prophecy of 2012），其閱讀重點如下：

① 2012 年末日預言的由來
② 末日預言的可信度

文章閱讀

Doomsday Prophecy of 2012

Many cultures around the world speak of a complete **destruction** of the world and sometimes they even capture the general public's imagination. The idea of 2012 being the end of the world is nothing new.

Many people believe that the Mayan calendar is due to end on 21st December 2012 and this will signal the end of the world. However, many serious academics of Mayan tradition explain that there is no evidence that Mayans thought the end of the calendar meant the end of the world. Research seems to **suggest** that they thought that once the cycle finished, another would begin.

The idea that the end of the calendar equals the end of the world has been around <u>since the mid 1970s</u> on "the fringe" of science and astronomy. Many scientists point to the fact that there is no special event scheduled to happen on that date. Much more significant events happened in space in 2000 and 2010 and yet, everybody was safe.

<u>Since the beginning of human existence,</u> we have **survived** many doomsday prophecies; another one will not kill us.

● 學習焦點 ···

自有人類文明以來，末日預言一直是大家關心的話題，本文從科學的觀點來探討馬雅曆法傳說，來消除世界末日的謠言。

① 第一段點出文章的立場："The idea of 2012 being the end of the world is nothing new."（2012 年是世界末日並非新鮮事）。

② 第二段說明馬雅曆書結束在 2012 年的十二月二十一日，因此當天被視為世界末日，但此說法缺乏實證（...there is no evidence...）；較可信的是：一旦一個周期結束，另一個會開始 "...once the cycle finished, another would begin."。

③ 第三段敘述末日的說法在 1970 年代中期，就遊走在科學和天文學的邊緣之間（...has been around since the mid 1970s on "the fringe" of science and astronomy.），但是曆書上看不出當日有任何特殊事件，反而是 2000 年及 2010 年在外太空曾發生更重大的事件（more significant events），人類卻安然無恙。

④ 作者在結語中奉勸大家不必對末日說太緊張，因為這類說法曾出現過很多次，
再多一個也不會毀滅人類（...another one will not kill us.）。

語言知識補充站 ···

★ Vocabulary

* doomsday prophecy
末日預言

* destruction：【名詞】毀滅；破壞
Many cultures around the world / speak of a complete destruction of the world
/ and sometimes they even / capture the general public's imagination.
世上許多文化 / 談論世界的全面毀滅 / 有時他們甚至 / 吸引一般大眾想像

* due：【修飾語】預期的；約定的
Many people believe / that the Mayan calendar / is due / to end on 21st
December 2012 / and this will signal / the end of the world.
許多人相信 / 馬雅曆書 / 預期 / 在 2012 年 12 月 21 日結束 / 這將標示 / 世界末日

* suggest：【動詞】暗示
用法：研究資料 + suggest + that + S + V
Research seems to suggest / that Mayans thought / that once the cycle finished,
/ another would begin.
研究似乎暗示 / 馬雅人認為 / 一旦一個周期結束 / 另一個將會開始

* survive：【動詞】倖存；比⋯⋯活得更久
用法：人 + survive + 災難事件
Since the beginning of human existence, / we / have survived many doomsday
prophecies; / another one / will not kill us.
自從有人類以來 / 我們 / 已經度過多次末日預言 / 另一個末日預言 / 不會毀滅我們

句型：S ＋ has／have ＋ V-ed ＋ since ＋ 過去的時間／過去發生的事件

本句型表達自從過去某個時間點或發生過某件事之後，就一直持續到現在的動作；請注意主要子句通常都是使用完成式 has／have ＋ V-ed。

① The idea that the end of the calendar equals the end of the world has been around since the mid 1970s on "the fringe" of science and astronomy.

　　表示「馬雅曆書終止那天就是世界末日」的這種想法，是從 1970 年代中期就開始，直到現在。

② Since the beginning of human existence, we have survived many doomsday prophecies

　　表示自從有人類以來，我們已經度過多次末日預言。

　🌑　摘要與測驗重點提示 ●●●

　★ 閱讀要項

本篇文章須要注意的重點如下：

① 敘述事情：doomsday prophecy of 2012
② 敘述重點：The end of the calendar does not equal the end of the world.
　　　　　　（曆書的結束並不等於世界的盡頭）

　★ 常用字彙及句法

① 暗示某種想法或概念：研究資料 ＋ suggest ＋ that ＋ S ＋ V

② 僥倖度過某種災變：人 + survive + 災難事件

★ 測驗重點

本文的重點資訊在於末日說的起源和內容，以及人們應有的態度。

練習題

1. What is the tone of the article?

a) Informative

b) Depressing

c) Descriptive

d) Exaggerated

2. What can be inferred from the article?

a) The world will end on 21st Dec. 2012.

b) Mayan calendar is the first sign of the end times.

c) Mayans probably thought that our world would enter another cycle after 21st Dec. 2012.

d) People created the Mayan calendar in the mid 1970s.

3. What would be another way to describe "the fringe" ?

a) At the forefront

b) At the centre

c) At the edge

d) In the future

The Doomsday Seed Vault

Have you ever thought about how we would grow plants if many of the world's crops died after a natural disaster? Well, at the Svalbard Global Seed Vault in Norway, they are collecting and preserving seeds for that reason and many others.

The seed vault currently has over 2 million seeds and has the capacity to hold 4.5 million. It is designed to keep the seed samples safe from natural and man-made disasters: global warming, asteroid strikes, plant diseases, nuclear warfare, and even earthquakes. It was built 120 meters inside a mountain in Spitsbergen. Because the weather is extremely cold there, the seeds are preserved by the freezing temperatures. The location is 130 meters above sea level, which means that the seeds will be safe even if the ice caps melt.

Construction of the seed vault, which cost approximately NOK 45 million (US$9 million), was funded entirely by the Government of Norway. Storage of seeds in the seed vault is free-of-charge. Operational costs are paid by Norway and the Global Crop Diversity Trust. Though Norway owns the global seed bank, the first of its kind, other countries can store seeds in it and remove them as needed.

1. What is the purpose of building the seed vault?

a) To prevent the seed samples from being destroyed

b) To breed seeds to create new varieties

c) To provide a shelter for people in case of war

d) To analyze plant diseases

2. What statement is true?

a) The vault is already overloaded with seed samples.

b) The construction of the vault was supported by the United Nations.

c) Storage of seeds in the seed vault is free of charge.

d) The storehouse will be flooded if the ice caps melt.

文章閱讀　翻譯與題解

2012 年末日預言

　　全球許多文化都謠傳相信世界將會完全毀滅，有時這些言論甚至吸引一般大眾的想像。而 2012 年將是世界末日的說法也已經不是新聞。

　　許多人相信因馬雅曆法只到 2012 年 12 月 21 日為止，而這象徵世界末日的到來。然而，許多嚴謹的馬雅傳統學術研究解釋道，並沒有證據足以證明馬雅人認為曆法的結束日就一定意味是世界末日來臨。研究似乎暗示，他們認為一旦一個周期結束，代表另一個周期即將開始。

　　曆法的結束等同於世界末日這樣的想法，從 1970 年代中期開始，就已經在科學與天文學的「邊緣」遊走並廣為流傳。許多科學家指出一項事實是：那天並沒有排定特殊活動，而且 2000 年到 2010 年間在外太空曾發生更重大的事件，但大家仍舊安然無恙。

　　自從人類存在以來，我們已經從許多末日預言中存活到現在；就算有另一個預言也殺不死我們了。

● 題解 ···

1. 解答：a) 傳達知識情報的

中譯：

這篇文章的用詞語氣為何？

a) 傳達知識情報的

b) 令人沮喪的

c) 記述性的

d) 誇大的

題解：由文章內容的描述方式可知，是在傳達知識性的訊息，故答案選 a)。

2. 解答：c) 馬雅人可能認為我們的世界將會在 2012 年 12 月 21 日之後進入另
一個周期。

中譯：

由這篇文章的描述可作下列哪項推論？

a) 世界將會在 2012 年 12 月 21 日走到盡頭。

b) 馬雅人的曆法是末日的第一個徵兆。

c) 馬雅人可能認為我們的世界將會在 2012 年 12 月 21 日之後進入另一個周期。

d) 人們在 1970 年代中期創造了馬雅曆法。

題解：由文章內容的描述可推知，選項 c) 正確。

3. 解答：c) 在邊緣

中譯：

要描述 "the fringe"（邊緣）可能有其他哪種方式？

a) 在最前線

b) 在中間

c) 在邊緣

d) 在未來

題解：由文章第三段內容可推知，"the fringe" 要表達的是在科學與天文學的邊
緣遊走，故答案選 c) 最貼切。

20

● 文章翻譯 ···

末日糧倉

　　你可曾試想過，如果有一天世界上的作物收成在一次天災後全部死光光，我們該如何繼續種植農作物呢？在挪威就有一個名為斯瓦爾巴的全球種子庫，他們為了上述原因及許多其他理由，進行種子的蒐集和保存工作。

　　該種子銀行目前擁有超過兩百萬顆種子，共能容納、保存約四百五十萬顆種子。這項設計是用來安全地保存種子的樣本，以防止天災及人禍：像是全球暖化、行星撞擊、植物病蟲害、核子戰爭、甚至是地震等災害的摧殘。它被建造在斯匹次卑爾根群島一座 120 公尺的山裡。因為那裡的氣候極度寒冷，種子可在其冰凍的溫度下保存良好。地點位在海拔一百三十公尺高的地方，這也意味著即使冰原溶化，這些種子仍會很安全。

　　種子銀行的建造由挪威政府全額資助，花費將近四千五百萬挪威克朗（約為九百萬美金）。將種子存放於種子銀行是免費的。營運成本由挪威政府及「全球作物多樣性信託」負擔。雖然挪威擁有全球種子銀行，也是第一家這類型的銀行，但其他國家也能將種子存放其中，並在需要時提領。

1. 解答：a) 避免種子樣本被摧毀

中譯：

建造種子銀行的目的為何？

a) 避免種子樣本被摧毀

b) 為了繁殖種子以創造新的品種

c) 以防戰爭爆發時，可以提供人們一個避難所

d) 為了分析植物的疾病

題解：文章第一段即說明成立種子庫的原因，目的是避免種子樣本因天災人禍而蕩然無存，故答案選 a)。

2. 解答：c) 在儲存庫內存放種子是免費的。

中譯：

下列哪一項敘述正確？

a) 儲存庫已經超過負荷，被種子的樣本塞爆。

b) 儲存庫的建設是由聯合國支持。

c) 在儲存庫內存放種子是免費的。

d) 如果冰原溶化，儲存庫將會被洪水淹沒。

題解：由文章第三段描述可知，將種子存放於糧倉內是免費的，故答案選 c)。

21

Wasting Time is the New Divide in the Digital Era
浪費時間是數位時代的新落差

㉑

閱讀重點 ....

本篇文章討論美國為了消弭貧富差距所造成的「數位落差」（digital divide），卻因此造成另一種「浪費時數」（wasting time）的新落差，其閱讀重點如下：

① 何謂「數位落差」與始料未及的新落差
② 造成新落差的原因

文章閱讀 ....

Wasting time is the New Divide in the Digital Era

　　In the 1990s, the term "digital divide" was created in the United States. It described the gap between people who had **access** to technology and those who did not. The solution was to make sure that all Americans, particularly low-income families, had access to computers.

　　This solution worked, but it also had an unexpected **negative** effect. Research has shown that children from poor families <u>spend more</u>

time watching TV and playing video games <u>than</u> children from wealthy families. You could also say that poor children waste more time. So the problem is not that the children don't have access to technology. The problem is that parents are unable to teach their children how to use technology in a good way.

Danah Boyd, a senior researcher at Microsoft, said that giving poor children access to computers does not solve anything. In fact, it simply  **shines a light on** existing problems – problems we have been ignoring. When researchers and policy makers tried to close the digital divide, they did not **foresee** how computers would be used for entertainment.

● 學習焦點 ••

本文敘述美國政府為了縮短貧富水準造成的數位落差,卻因為決策者在規畫時的疏忽,使得此政策的一番美意變成另一種新的落差。

① 第一段說明所謂的「數位落差」是描述 1990 年代的美國,使用科技設備的人和未使用者間的落差(the gap between people who had access to technology and those who did not);解決之道是確保所有家庭都有電腦可用,尤其是低收入戶(particularly low-income families)。

② 接著以一句話轉折第一段的語氣:解決方案居然出現意外的負面效應(an unexpected negative effect)。

③ 第三段解釋負面效應產生的現象與原因:貧窮家庭的小孩比富有家庭的小孩浪費更多時間在電玩上,形成所謂的新落差(new divide);原因是低收入的父母無法教導小孩如何善用科技(...parents are unable to teach their children how to use technology in a good way.)。

21

④ 第四段批判決策過程的盲點："When researchers and policy makers tried to close the digital divide, they did not foresee how computers would be used for entertainment."（研究人員與政策擬定者試圖縮小數位差距時，並未預見電腦的娛樂用途。）。

🌐 語言知識補充站 ⋯⋯⋯⋯⋯⋯⋯⋯⋯⋯⋯⋯⋯⋯⋯⋯⋯⋯⋯⋯⋯⋯

★ Vocabulary

＊ divide：【名詞】落差；分歧

In the 1990s, / the term "digital divide" / was created / in the United States.
在 1990 年代 /「數位落差」這個術語 / 被創造出來 / 在美國

＊ access：【名詞】接近的機會；進入的權利

用法：access to ＋ 資源／設施

The solution was / to make sure / that all Americans, / particularly low-income families, / had access to computers.
解決之道是 / 確認 / 所有美國人 / 尤其是低收入戶 / 可以接觸電腦

＊ negative：【修飾詞】負面的；否定的

This solution worked, / but / it also had an unexpected negative effect.
解決方案生效了 / 但是 / 它也有意外的負面效應

＊ shine a light on：揭露（某問題）

用法：shine a light on ＋ 問題／現象

It simply / shines a light on existing problems / – problems we have been ignoring.
它僅僅是 / 顯露早已存在的問題 / 我們一直忽略的問題

＊ foresee：【動詞】預知；預見

When researchers and policy makers / tried to close the digital divide, / they / did not foresee / how computers would be used for entertainment.

當研究人員和政策擬定者 / 企圖縮短數位落差 / 他們 / 並沒有預見 / 電腦是如何作為娛樂用途

★ Sentence Pattern

句型：S_1 ＋ V ＋ more ＋（名詞）＋ than ＋ S_2

這種句型常用來比較兩者（S_1 與 S_2）之間的差異，more 在此用來修飾後面的名詞，表示 S_1 的動作造成更多的特質或事物（名詞）。

Children from poor families spend more time watching TV and playing video games than children from wealthy families.

表示主詞一（children from poor families）花費（spend）更多時間（time）在看電視和打電動玩具。

摘要與測驗重點提示 ●●●●●●●●●●●●●●●●●●●●●●●●●●●●●●●●●●●●

★ 閱讀要項

本篇文章須要注意的重點如下：

① 敘述主題：the new divide in the digital era
② 現象：Children from poor families spend more time watching TV and playing video games than children from wealthy families.
③ 原因：The problem is that parents are unable to teach their children how to use technology in a good way.

① 表示能接觸或使用某設施：用法：access to ＋ 資源 / 設施
② 揭露某個問題：shine a light on ＋ 問題 / 現象
③ 比較兩者之間的差異：S_1 ＋ V ＋ more ＋（名詞）＋ than ＋ S_2

★ 測驗重點

本文的重點資訊在於光有使用科技的機會是不夠的，還要具備善用科技的能力才行。

練習題

1. What is the main cause of the growing time-wasting gap?

a) Low-income parents don't know how to control their children's Internet use.

b) Children in poorer families have limited access to the Internet.

c) Policy makers don't know how to decrease the gap.

d) Children from wealthy families spend less time watching television.

2. What do researchers think about the time-wasting gap?

a) They had foreseen this problem before the 1990s.

b) They think that access is the only solution to this gap.

c) They never expected this effect to happen.

d) They will make more efforts to close the digital divide.

Resist the Urge to Quit

How often do we set goals in our life, then quit before we reach them? Working towards a goal can be hard. It requires effort. Often we are afraid of failure. Sometimes we are even afraid of success. Here are some suggestions to help you keep going.

1. Focus on Today

Don't think too much about the future. You don't have to achieve your goal straight away. Just focus on today, and take a small step.

2. Take Action

The smallest action can bring back your passion for your goal. That passion will keep you going through the hard times.

3. Look at How Far You've Come

Take a moment to look back and see how far you have come. It's really motivating to see that you are actually making progress!

4. Do One Thing Differently

Albert Einstein said: Insanity is doing the same thing many times and expecting a different result. Sometimes one small change can make a huge difference in our lives.

5. Forget About the Outcome

When we forget about the outcome, we are less afraid of failure. That makes it easier to keep moving towards our goal.

6. Remember Your Passion

Remind yourself why this goal is so important to you. Remember that you are working hard for something you really want.

練習題

1. What is the main purpose of this article?

a) To tell people the importance of goal setting

b) To tell people the good side about today

c) To encourage people to work toward their goals

d) To teach people how to let go of fear

2. What can be inferred from Albert Einstein's definition of insanity?

a) A successful person will always follow the same pattern.

b) A small change can open a new page in your life.

c) Practice makes perfect.

d) You can get what you want in the end.

文章閱讀 翻譯與題解

● 文章翻譯

浪費時間是數位時代的新落差

1990 年代的美國,「數位落差」這個詞彙被創造出來。用來描述那些使用科技設備的人和未使用者間的落差。這個問題的解決之道,是確保所有美國人,特別是低收入家庭,有機會能接觸到電腦。

這個方法果真奏效,但也帶來意料之外的負面效果。

研究顯示來自貧困家庭的孩子比起富裕家庭的小孩,會花更多時間在看電視和玩電玩遊戲。這也可以解釋成貧困家庭的小孩浪費了更多的時間。所以問題的癥結不在於孩子們沒有接觸到科技,而在於父母未能教導孩子們如何善用科技。

微軟的資深研究員——丹納 · 波伊德說道:讓貧窮家庭的兒童能接觸到電腦並未解決任何問題。事實上這正凸顯了我們一直忽略的現有問題。當研究人員和政策制定者試圖縮小數位落差時,他們並未預見電腦將如何應用在娛樂方面。

題解 ••

1. 解答：a) 低收入家庭的父母不知道如何控制孩子的網路使用方式。

中譯：

時間浪費落差增加的主要原因是什麼？

a) 低收入家庭的父母不知道如何控制孩子的網路使用方式。

b) 出生在較貧困家庭的孩子，使用網際網路較受限。

c) 政策制定者不知道如何降低這個落差。

d) 富裕家庭的孩子花較少時間看電視。

題解：由文章第一段到第三段的描述可推知，文章作者認為低收入家庭的父母未能教導孩子們如何善用科技、掌控使用的時間，故選 a)。

2. 解答：c) 他們從未預期會發生這樣的影響。

中譯：

研究人員如何看待時間浪費落差的問題？

a) 他們在 1990 年代之前即已預見這個問題。

b) 他們認為使用電腦是解決這個落差的唯一方法。

c) 他們從未預期會發生這樣的影響。

d) 他們會更努力縮小數位落差。

題解：由文章第二段可知，想出解決之道的人，並未預期會帶來負面影響，故答案選 c)。

● 文章翻譯 ···

抗拒放棄的衝動

人生中我們是不是常常設定了目標，卻在達成前就放棄了這個目標呢？朝目標奮鬥的確不易。那需要付出努力。我們常會害怕失敗，有時，甚至也害怕成功。下面有些建議可以幫助你勇往直前：

1. 專注在當下

別總是想著未來，你不必立即達成目標。只要專注在當下，一步一腳印。

2. 採取行動

微小的行動也可以令你重拾對目標的熱忱。那份熱情會帶你克服艱難的時刻繼續前進。

3. 看看你已經前進了多少

花些時間回顧，看看你已經做了多少。如果能看到自己的確有進步，著實會讓人充滿動力。

4. 同樣的事，不同做法

亞伯特‧愛因斯坦曾說道：「瘋狂就是重複做同樣的事情，卻期望得到不同的結果。」有時候一個小改變就可以創造人生的大不同。

21

5. 不去想結果

如果我們不刻意去設想結果，就比較不會害怕失敗。這樣會較容易督促自己繼續往目標邁進。

6. 牢記你的熱情

提醒自己為什麼這個目標對你而言如此重要。要記得你正為自己真正想要的目標使盡全力。

 題解 ···

1. 解答：c) 鼓勵人們朝自己的目標努力

中譯：

本文的主旨為何？

a) 告訴人們訂立目標的重要性

b) 告訴人們今日的光明面

c) 鼓勵人們朝自己的目標努力

d) 教導人們如何放下恐懼

題解：從本文的標題及內容各要點可知，主要在鼓勵人們朝自己的目標邁進，故答案選 c)。

2. 解答：b) 一個小改變可以開啟人生的新頁。

中譯：

從愛因斯坦對瘋狂的定義可以推論出下列何者？

a) 成功者總是會追隨相同的典範。

b) 一個小改變可以開啟人生的新頁。

c) 熟能生巧。

d) 最終你可以如願以償。

題解：由文中第四點末句可知，答案選 b) 最貼切。

職場應用篇

22

5 Body Language Signals
That Will Ruin Your Interview
面試五禁忌

22

閱讀重點

本篇文章是討論面試（interview）的時候，須要避免的不適當肢體語言（body language），其閱讀重點如下：

① 肢體語言的重要性
② 五種不恰當的肢體語言

文章閱讀

Body Language Signals That Will Ruin Your Interview

Nobody should be surprised that how you behave is just as important as what you actually say in an interview. Here are the five most common body language mistakes people make in an interview:

1. Properly shaking hands will create a good **impression**. Make sure your handshake is firm – you <u>don't</u> want to crush the other person's hand, <u>nor</u> do you want to hold it gently like a

dead fish. Also, make sure your hand is dry. A sweaty hand is a handshake's worst nightmare.

2. Don't touch your face. For the interviewer, touching your face could be seen as a sign that you are not telling the truth.

3. Don't fold your arms. Doing this is often interpreted as a sign of defensiveness and passive aggressiveness. As we want to **demonstrate** assertiveness, it would be better to put your hands on the table where they can't cause any problems.

4. Don't stare. There's a difference between positive eye contact and plain staring. Of course you should **maintain** some eye contact, but do not let it degenerate into uncomfortable staring. At the same time, don't let your eyes wander around the room as if you're bored.

5. Avoid nodding too much. Like eye contact, nod **moderately**, and only when it's clearly suitable.

● 學習焦點 ••

本文先說明一般人在面談時的肢體表現跟口頭回答的內容是一樣重要,再列舉五種最常見的不當肢體語言。

① 第一句點出肢體動作與口說內容一樣重要 "...how you behave is just as important as what you actually say in a job interview."。接著說明哪些是最常見的錯誤肢體語言。

② "Properly shaking hands will create a good impression."(適度地握手會製造好印象):力道拿捏要恰好,太重,會傷了對方的手(crush the other person's hand),太輕則像條死魚(like a dead fish)。

22

③ "Don't touch your face." （別碰觸你的臉）：碰觸臉龐會讓別人覺得你沒說真話。

④ "Don't fold your arms." （不要交疊雙臂）：這個動作有兩個含意，一為自我防禦（defensiveness），二為消極的挑釁（passive aggressiveness）；如果不想製造麻煩，把雙手放在桌上會比較好。

⑤ "Don't stare." （別瞪著人看）：面試時適度的眼神交會（eye contact）是必要的，但不能變成死盯著對方；眼神也不要四處飄移，表現出無聊的樣子。

⑥ "Avoid nodding too much." （避免過度點頭）：同眼神交會般，應點到為止。

🌀 語言知識補充站 ……………………………………………………………

★ Vocabulary

＊ interview：【名詞】面談
How you behave / is just as important as / what you actually say / in an interview.
你的行為舉止 / 與……等同重要 / 你真正說出的話 / 在工作面試中

＊ impression：【名詞】印象
用法：人 + create a + 修飾詞 + impression
Properly shaking hands / will create / a good impression.
適當地握手 / 將會製造 / 一個好的印象

＊ demonstrate：【動詞】展現；表示
用法：人 + demonstrate + 某種個人特質
As we want to demonstrate assertiveness, / it would be better / to put your hands on the table / where they can't cause any problems.
因為我們要展現自信 / 會比較好 / 把你的手放在桌上 / 他們不會引起任何問題的地方

＊maintain：【動詞】維持

You should maintain / some eye contact, / but do not let it degenerate into / uncomfortable staring.

你應該維持 / 一些眼神交會 / 但不要讓它變成 / 令人不自在的瞪視

＊moderately：【修飾語】有節制地，適度地

Like eye contact, / nod moderately, / and only when it's clearly suitable.

如同眼神交會一樣 / 適度地點頭 / 只有確定在合適的時候

★ Sentence Pattern

句型：S + do / does / did + not + V$_1$, nor + do / does / did + S + V$_2$

雙重否定是英文特有的句型，用來強調主詞不想做這件事（V$_1$），也不想做另一件事（V$_2$）；請注意逗點後面的 nor 是以倒裝句（do / does / did 放在主詞前面）方式呈現。

You <u>don't</u> want to crush the other person's hand, <u>nor</u> do you want to hold it gently like a dead fish.

表示主詞 you 不想壓碎（crush）別人的手，也不想像條死魚般握著（hold）對方。

摘要與測驗重點提示 ●●●●●●●●●●●●●●●●●●●●●●●●●●●●●●●●●●

★ 閱讀要項

本篇文章須要注意的重點如下：

① 描述對象：interviewee（接受面試的人）
② 敘述重點：five most common body language mistakes

22

① 表現個人特質的常用動詞：demonstrate, maintain
② 說明給予他人的印象：人 ＋ create a ＋ 修飾詞＋ impression

★ 測驗重點

本文的重點資訊在於當心面試時的肢體語言，並指出五種常見的錯誤。

練習題

1. What kind of body language will make the interviewer think that you can't be trusted?

a) Nodding your head

b) Sweaty handshakes

c) Keeping eye contact

d) Touching your face

2. Which non-verbal gesture is recommended during an interview?

a) A perfect resume

b) Answering all the questions

c) Putting your hands on the table

d) An aggressive handshake

Top 5 Things You Should NEVER Say During a Job Interview

There are many things that you should not talk about during a job interview. Five of the worst are listed below.

1. How much is the salary?

   The interviewer might think that all you are after is money.

2. What does your company make (or do)?

   A prospective candidate must do research on the company before the job interview.

3. I don't have any weaknesses.

   Everyone has strengths and weaknesses. If you say you only have strengths, the interviewer will decide that you are either lying or that you are not thinking.

4. Do not criticize any former employer.

   Criticism of a previous boss lets the interviewer know that you will do the same to them if you leave their company. Alternatively, you can explain that you and your former employer had different opinions with regard to working practices.

5. Will I have to work overtime?

   A much better idea would be to ask what a typical workday is like. You'll get a good idea of workload and daily hours without seeming inflexible.

1. 1. Why shouldn't you criticize a former boss?

a) It shows you had a different opinion.

b) You will leave the company.

c) It suggests you may do the same if you leave.

d) Your former boss had different working habits.

2. Why should you NOT ask about the salary?

a) It makes you look bored.

b) It shows you are not interested.

c) It shows that you earn enough.

d) It shows that you are only interested in how much you earn.

● 文章翻譯

面試五禁忌

不可否認的，工作面試時的肢體動作和實際表達的話語內容一樣重要。下面舉出五種在面試時，人們最常出現的錯誤肢體語言：

1. 適度握手寒暄可以給人留下好印象。必須確認你握手的方式是堅定的—並非用力擠壓握斷對方的手，也不是像條死魚般軟弱無力。此外，要確保你的手是乾的。用汗手與人交握是最糟糕的惡夢。
2. 別碰觸自己的臉。對面試人員來說，碰觸臉頰可能被視為你沒在說真話的象徵。
3. 不要交疊雙臂。這麼做的話通常會被理解成具防禦性和消極挑釁的象徵。如果你想表現自信，最佳的作法是將雙手放在桌面，就不會引起任何不必要的誤會。
4. 不要瞪著對方。正確自信的眼神交會與漠然無神的呆視有很大不同。面試時當然必需保持一些眼神交會，但不要流於盯著對方看，令人感到不舒服。同時，也不要眼神四處飄移好像你覺得很無聊的樣子。
5. 避免一直點頭。如同眼神交會，只有在明顯合適的情況下，適度地點頭回應即可。

題解

1. 解答：d) 摸自己的臉

中譯：

下列哪一種肢體語言會讓面試官認為你不值得信任？

a) 點頭示意

b) 用汗手與人交握

c) 保持眼神交會

d) 摸自己的臉

題解：如同文章中提到的第二點，摸著自己的臉會讓面試官覺得這個人在說謊，故答案 d) 最恰當。

2. 解答：c) 將雙手置於桌面

中譯：

在面試時，建議採取下列哪項非語言的肢體動作？

a) 一份完美的履歷

b) 回答所有問題

c) 將雙手置於桌面

d) 用力地握手

題解：文章中第三點建議，將雙手置於桌面可以表現自信，又不會引起不必要的肢體語言誤會，故答案選 c)。

● 文章翻譯

面試時不能說的祕密

有許多事情不該在工作面試時談論。最糟糕的前五項如下所列：

1. 薪水是多少？

   可能會讓面試官認為你最在乎的只有錢。

2. 貴公司是做什麼的？

   一個有企圖進入該公司工作的求職者，應該在面試前針對該公司蒐集資料。

3. 說自己沒有任何缺點。

   每個人都有優缺點。如果你說自己只有優點，會讓面試官認為你不是在說謊，不然就是你根本沒在用腦袋思考。

4. 切勿批評任何前雇主。

   批評前老闆只會讓面試官認定，如果你離開他們公司，也會這樣批評他們。相對地，你可解釋你和你的前雇主對於工作業務有不同的見解。

5. 我需要加班嗎？

   較佳的詢問方式是問一般的工時是如何？如此可以得知工作量和每日平均工時，而不會顯得你這個人缺乏彈性。

1. 解答：c) 那會讓人認為如果你離職也會這樣批評他們。

中譯：

為什麼應試者面試時不該批評前老闆？

a) 那顯示你跟老闆有不同見解。

b) 表示你會離職。

c) 那會讓人認為如果你離職也會這樣批評他們。

d) 表示你的前老闆與你有著不同的工作習慣。

題解：由文章提到的第四點可知，在面試官面前批評前老闆，會造成如選項 c) 描述的負面聯想。

2. 解答：d) 顯示你只對可以賺多少錢感興趣。

中譯：

面試時為什麼不宜問薪水？

a) 會讓你這個人看來很無趣。

b) 顯示你對這份工作不感興趣。

c) 顯示你已經賺夠了。

d) 顯示你只對可以賺多少錢感興趣。

題解：由文章提到的第一點可知，主動問薪水多少，會讓人覺得你只在乎賺多少錢，故答案選 d)。

23

How to Get Your Boss to Give You a Raise
「薪事」誰人知

閱讀重點

本篇文章是討論如何主動出擊，要求老闆幫你加薪（ask for a pay raise），其閱讀重點如下：

① 不要被動等待，必須採取主動、要求加薪。
② 有助於達到加薪目標的六個祕訣。

文章閱讀

How to Get Your Boss to Give You a Raise

Sitting and waiting for your boss to give you a raise hasn't worked so far. What are you waiting for? It's time to ask for a raise. Here are some tips to help.

1. Take a mature approach. When it comes to asking for a raise, the best way is to ask for extra work and **responsibility** and link this to a pay raise.

2. Record things you've done for the company. This shows you deserve a raise.
3. Research the **average** salary in your profession. What salary range is consistent with your work experience and performance?
4. Look at all your options. For example, your employer might give you more vacation time or further training. Consider options other than more money.
5. Make an appointment with your employer. The request for a raise should be **treated** like a formal meeting.
6. Go to the appointment and **remain** calm when talking about a pay raise. Use the arguments listed above.

Your career is a marathon, not a sprint. Take a long-term perspective and have faith that you will get what you deserve.

● 學習焦點 ••

若想擁有更好的待遇必須主動出擊，本文列舉六種有助於成功加薪的祕訣。

① 第一句點出被動等待，並無益於加薪，鼓勵大家現在是主動要求加薪的好時機 "It's time to ask for a raise."；接著提出六種加薪祕技。

② 最好的方法是主動承擔更多工作，讓加薪順理成章 "the best way is to ask for extra work and responsibility and link this to a pay raise."。

③ "Record things you've done for the company."（記錄你為公司做過的事情），讓老闆知道你該享有更好的待遇。

④ "Research the average salary in your profession."（研究同業的平均薪資水準）：找出符合你條件的職位薪資幅度。

⑤ "Look at all your options."（審視你可能的各種選項）：除了金錢以外，也可以考慮其他替代方案，例如休假或訓練（more vacation time or further training）。

⑥ "Make an appointment with your employer."（與你的雇主約時間）：加薪是很嚴肅的議題，要如同正式的會議般看待。

⑦ "Go to the appointment and remain calm when talking about a pay raise."（赴約時，用冷靜的態度討論你的薪水）：使用以上論點來幫助你達到目標。

💬 語言知識補充站 ••

★ **Vocabulary**

* raise：【名詞】提高；加薪
Sitting and waiting for your boss / to give you a raise / hasn't worked / so far.
坐著等待你的老闆 / 給你加薪 / 並不會產生效果 / 到目前為止

* responsibility：【名詞】責任
When it comes to / asking for a raise, / the best way is / to ask for extra work and responsibility / and link this to a pay raise.
每當談到 / 要求加薪 / 最好的方式是 / 要求額外工作和責任 / 將此與加薪結合在一起

* average：【修飾語】平均的
Research / the average salary / in your profession.
研究 / 平均薪資水準 / 在你的同業中

* treat：【動詞】對待；看待

用法：事物 $_1$ ＋ be treated like ＋ 事物 $_2$

The request for a raise / should be treated / like a formal meeting.

加薪請求 / 應該被看成 / 如同正式會議一般

* remain：【動詞】保持

用法：人 / 事物 ＋ remain ＋ 表示狀態的修飾詞

Go to the appointment / and remain calm / when talking about a pay raise.

準時赴約 / 保持冷靜 / 談到有關加薪的事情

★ Sentence Pattern

句型：When it comes to ＋ 人 / 事物 / V-ing, S ＋ V

本句型的意思是當談話或寫文章，提到某個主題時，藉此延伸作者對這個主題的看法或態度。

When it comes to asking for a raise, the best way is to ask for extra work and responsibility and link this to a pay raise.

表示每當談到要求加薪時，作者認為最佳方式就是要求額外的工作和責任，並與加薪這個議題結合在一起。

摘要與測驗重點提示 ●●●

★ 閱讀要項

本篇文章須要注意的重點如下：

① 描述對象：people who want a raise （想要加薪的人）
② 敘述重點：six tips to help you to ask for a raise. （六個幫助你加薪的祕訣）

① 事物如何被看待：事物₁ + be treated like + 事物₂
② 表示人或物的狀態：人 / 事物 + remain + 表示狀態的修飾詞
③ 每當提到某個主題：When it comes to + 人 / 事物 / V-ing, S + V

★ 測驗重點

本文的重點資訊在於主動出擊和成功加薪的祕訣。

練習題

1. Why should you record your contributions?

a) It will give your boss something to do.

b) It can be used as evidence of your performance.

c) It will increase your workload.

d) It can be used for research.

2. What should you not do when asking for a raise?

a) Be willing to shoulder more responsibility.

b) Compare your salary with that of others in the same field.

c) Treat the request as a casual get-together.

d) Consider non-monetary options.

3. What is the meaning of "a marathon, not a sprint" ?

a) It is a long, not a short experience.

b) It is a short, not a long experience.

c) It is good to exercise at work.

d) You should run for a raise.

23

Convince Your Boss to Let You Work from Home

According to a report, people spend more than 328 hours traveling to work every year. If you can convince your employer to let you work from home one day per week, you'd save over eight work days of time for the whole year. Here are some tips to help you do that.

1. Make sure you understand what technology is required to work from home. For example, can you access companywide software from home?
2. Become an ideal employee, so your boss feels you would do just as much work without someone watching you.
3. Focus on business benefits and minimize personal benefits. Remind your boss of advantages like attracting and retaining valuable workers, saving on parking, or being environmentally-friendly.
4. Start by suggesting a trial of one day per week for 5 or 6 weeks.
5. Create a successful trial period. Once your boss agrees, you aren't free and clear. Keep regular tabs on how things progress at work and keep things running smoothly.

Working at home isn't for everyone, but it can be a way to reclaim time lost to commuting.

1. What kind of employee does NOT qualify for working from home?

a) A person who can access his/her file from home

b) A person who will concentrate on the job

c) A person who only focuses on personal benefits

d) A person who contacts his/her supervisor on a regular basis

2. In this case, what is an example of a "personal benefit" ?

a) Employee retention rate

b) Environmental concerns

c) More vacation time

d) Saving parking space

文章閱讀 翻譯與題解

● 文章翻譯 ....

「薪事」誰人知

　　坐在那等著老闆替你加薪的想法並不可行。既然如此，你還等什麼呢？主動要求加薪的時候到了！以下是達成這個目標的小訣竅：

1. 採取穩重保守的方式。說到要求加薪，最佳作法是主動承擔額外的工作與責任，並以此跟加薪這件事搭上關係。
2. 記錄下你為公司完成的工作事項。藉此顯示替你加薪是值得的。
3. 研究同業的平均薪資水準。計算怎樣的薪資幅度能符合你的工作經驗和表現。
4. 審視你目前可有的選項。舉例來說，你的主管也許可以讓你放更多的假，或是提供更進一步的教育訓練。考慮一下金錢以外的獎勵方式。
5. 和主管預約時間。請求加薪應該要像開會討論一樣正式。
6. 準時赴約，並在討論加薪時保持心平氣和。善加運用上面所列幾點理由，努力爭取。

　　你的職涯就像一場長期的馬拉松賽跑，而非短暫的衝刺。必須站在長遠的角度思考，並相信你可以獲得應得的報償。

1. 解答：b) 這可以作為你個人表現的依據。

中譯：

為什麼要記錄你對公司的貢獻？

a) 如此一來可以讓你的老闆有事可做。

b) 這可以作為你個人表現的依據。

c) 這會增加你的工作量。

d) 這可以作為研究之用。

題解：由文章中所列的加薪小訣竅之第二點推知，這項記錄可以作為說服老闆替你加薪的具體證明，故答案選 b)。

2. 解答：c) 將要求加薪的場合，視作非正式的聚會。

中譯：

要求加薪時有什麼不可犯的禁忌？

a) 自願承擔較多的責任。

b) 和相同領域的人比較一下薪資幅度。

c) 將要求加薪的場合，視作非正式的聚會。

d) 考慮非金錢的獎酬方式。

題解：由文章中提醒的第五點可知，跟主管談加薪，需要像開會一樣，先跟主管預約時間，很正式地提出你的依據和訴求，不可隨便，故答案選 c)。

3. 解答：a) 這是一個長遠而非短暫的經驗。

中譯：

「像一場長期的馬拉松賽跑，而非短暫的衝刺」這句話的含義為何？

a) 這是一個長遠而非短暫的經驗。

b) 這是一個短暫而非長遠的經驗。

c) 工作時做運動是件好事。

d) 為了加薪你必須奔跑。

題解：由文章內容可以推知，文末這句話的意思是，必須站在長遠的角度來思考加薪這件事，故答案選 a)。

23

● 文章翻譯 ∙∙∙

說服你的主管讓你在家工作

根據一篇報告指出，每年人們花超過 328 小時的時間通勤上班。如果能夠說服你的主管一週有一天讓你在家工作，一整年可以省下超過八天的工作時間。在此提供一些可以幫忙達成這個目標的小訣竅：

1. 確認具備在家工作所需的設備和技術。舉例來說，你可以在家連線使用全公司的軟體嗎？
2. 成為一位模範員工。如此一來，你的老闆才會相信，即使在主管看不到的狀況下，你也會同樣盡責工作。
3. 把在家工作的好處聚焦在公司利益，而非個人私益上。提醒你的老闆這麼做的好處，像是可以吸引並留住有價值的員工，也可節省停車費，對環境而言也較環保。
4. 一開始先建議老闆讓你一週在家工作一天，連續試辦五到六週看看。
5. 創造一段成功的試辦期。一旦老闆同意，你並不是就放假解脫，而要規律地回報工作進度，並讓事情順利進行。

在家工作並非人人適用，但是個可以改善耗費通勤時間問題的方式。

1. 解答：c) 只在意個人利益的員工

中譯：

哪一類型的員工不符合在家工作的條件？

a) 在家可以順利使用資料、檔案的員工

b) 即使在家也可以專注於工作的員工

c) 只在意個人利益的員工

d) 會主動固定與主管聯絡的員工

題解：由文章內容可知，只在意個人私益的員工無法說服老闆讓他在家工作，而其他選項均符合可在家工作的條件，故答案選 c)。

2. 解答：c) 更多的假期

中譯：

承上題，如此一來，下列哪項是屬於為了「個人私益」的例子？

a) 員工的留職率

b) 環境考量因素

c) 更多的假期

d) 省下停車空間

題解：由文章中第三點的描述可知，選項 c) 所指即為個人私益。

24

Help Wanted
徵人啟事

㉔

閱讀重點 ●●●

公司行號或其他組織有職缺（job opening）時，會先刊登徵才廣告（want ad），本文以招募社會服務的主管為例，其閱讀重點如下：

① 職位名稱：Social Service Director
② 人選特質：leadership and team building skills
③ 學經歷條件：a Bachelor's degree and supervisor experience

文章閱讀 ●●●

Help Wanted

Social Service Director

Bring your leadership and team building skills to the Newstead Foundation. The exceptional community leader we seek is able to create close and lasting relationships with community members. To succeed, you must have a Bachelor's degree in social work or a related field and have at least 1 year of experience as a supervisor.

Please send resume and salary requirements to:
Mae Barrett, Administrator
Newstead Foundation
123 First St.
Newstead, NC 92846

🔵 學習焦點 ···

本文標題 "Help Wanted"（徵人啟事）及第二行的 "Social Service Director"，
清楚點出文章的目的，接下來的部份就在說明這個職位需要的特質和條件。

① 第一句以 "Bring your leadership and team building skills to the Newstead
  Foundation." 點出該職位需要 leadership（領導能力）與組織團隊能力（team
  building skills）。

② 第二句解釋該職位的工作目標："to create close and lasting relationships
  with community members"（和社區成員營造出親密且長久的關係）。

③ 第三句列出應徵的資格："a Bachelor's degree in social work or a related
  field and have at least 1 year of experience as a supervisor."（社福工作或相
  關領域的學士學位，而且至少一年擔任管理者的經驗）。

④ 最後告知如何應徵與聯絡人 "Please send resume and salary requirements
  to…"。

★ **Vocabulary**

＊ skill：【名詞】技能；能力

Bring your leadership / and team building skills / to the Newstead Foundation.

帶著你的領導才能 / 和組織團隊能力 / 到 Newstead 基金會。

＊ exceptional：【修飾語】特殊的；優秀的

用法：exceptional ＋ 職位名稱 / 某種專業能力

The exceptional community leader / we seek / is able to create / close and lasting relationships / with community members.

優秀的社區領導者 / 我們所尋求的 / 是能夠創造 / 親密和持久的關係 / 與社區成員。

＊ supervisor：【名詞】管理者

To succeed, / you must have a Bachelor's degree / in social work or a related field / and have at least 1 year of experience / as a supervisor.

想成功 / 你必須有學士學位 / 在社會福利工作或相關領域 / 而且具備至少一年的經驗 / 擔任管理者

＊ requirement：【名詞】必要條件

Please / send / resume and salary requirements / to the following address.

請 / 寄 / 履歷和希望待遇 / 到下述地址

句型：To V, S + V

由 **To -V** 所開頭的片語，是表達含有「為了某些目的或達到某些目的……」的意思，由主要句子的動作來完成這些目的。

<u>To succeed</u>, you must have a Bachelor's degree in social work or a related field and have at least 1 year of experience as a supervisor.

To succeed 表示目的，要是想成功，你（主詞）必須有社會福利或相關領域的學士學位，和至少一年的管理經驗。

摘要與測驗重點提示 ⋯⋯⋯⋯⋯⋯⋯⋯⋯⋯⋯⋯⋯⋯⋯⋯

★ 閱讀要項

徵才廣告屬於應用文體，都是以直接、明確的文字說明以下必要資訊：

① 職缺名稱：social service director
② 招募單位：Newstead Foundation
③ 人選特質：leadership and team building skills
④ 申請資格：a Bachelor's degree and supervisor experience
⑤ 聯絡方式：send resume and salary requirements to Mae Barrett, Administrator, Newstead Foundation, 123 First St. Newstead, NC 92846

★ 常用字彙及句法

① 描述專業能力或特質：leadership（領導才能）、team building skill（團隊建立能力）、exceptional（優秀的）

Help Wanted　徵人啟事

職場應用篇

24

265

② 敘述資格或條件：degree（學位）、field（領域）、requirement（要求）

★ 測驗重點

本文章的重點資訊在於想要找什麼樣的人才，包括人選的特質以及申請該工作的資格。

練習題

1. What kind of person is being sought?

a) Someone who is research-oriented

b) Someone with a Ph. D. in Social Work

c) A sports trainer

d) A leader

2. How can one apply for the job?

a) Mail a résumé.

b) Apply in person.

c) Call for an interview.

d) Log on to the company's Website.

Help Wanted

The Daily Gregorian, Inc. is looking for high-energy people to sell subscriptions to our newspaper. The Daily Gregorian has been faithfully reporting the news to this area for over 60 years, as well as providing the finest possible forum for public comment, community announcements and advertisements from local businesses.

If you have a good personality, you can make a commission on top of an hourly wage merely by speaking with people about our newspaper. There are two types of positions — telephone sales and door-to-door sales.

Most people in this community who are not current subscribers have merely let their subscriptions end, and are waiting for someone to contact them and take the hassle out of re-subscribing. You could be that person if you are over the age of 18. If this work appeals to you, please contact us by email at Gregorian@fullcom.com.

1. Which description best fits this job?

a) Hiring newspaper workers

b) Selling newspaper subscriptions

c) Selling newspaper advertisements

d) Advertising newspaper subscriptions

2. What is the only requirement for applicants?

a) A bright personality

b) More than 18 years old

c) Able to walk from door to door

d) A very hard worker

文章閱讀 翻譯與題解

● 文章翻譯 ....

徵人啟事

徵社會服務督導

　　歡迎具備領導長才和團隊合作技巧的你加入「Newstead 基金會」。我們在尋找一位出色的社區督導,能長期經營並和社區居民建立密切的關係。 要勝任這份工作,您必須擁有社工或相關領域之學士學歷,並需具備至少一年以上的管理經驗。

　　請將您的履歷及期望薪資待遇寄到以下地址:

Mae Barrett 主任　收

Newstead 基金會

北卡羅萊納州紐斯第市第一街 123 號

1. 解答：d) 主管

中譯：

他們在徵求哪種人才？

a) 研究導向的人才

b) 擁有社工博士學位的人

c) 運動教練

d) 主管

題解：由標題中的 director 和第二句中的關鍵字 leader、leadership 推斷，他們在找一位具領導能力的主管，故答案選 d)。

2. 解答：a) 郵寄履歷

中譯：

要如何應徵這份工作？

a) 郵寄履歷。

b) 親自去應徵。

c) 打電話去面試。

d) 登入該公司的網站。

題解：由末尾關鍵句 "Please send résumé and salary requirements to…" 和後面所附的郵寄地址推知，應用郵寄履歷的方式應徵，故選 a)。

徵人啟事

　　格里高日報正在招募充滿活力的訂報業務員。過去六十多年來，格里高日報忠實報導本地新聞，並闢有民意論壇、社區公告及本地商家廣告等版面。

　　若您個性開朗，只要靠口頭推銷本報就可賺取時薪外加佣金。現在我們提供兩種職位—電話行銷與拜訪銷售業務。

　　本社區裡有許多非本報訂戶的居民，多數是在訂閱到期後等著專人前往接洽，以省去續訂的麻煩。若您已年滿十八歲，您可能就是我們在尋覓的人選。若您對這項工作有興趣，請透過電子郵件與我們連絡：Gregorian@fullcom.com。

1. 解答：b) 推銷報紙訂閱

中譯：

下列哪個描述最符合此工作內容？

a) 雇用派報生

b) 推銷報紙訂閱

c) 推銷報紙廣告刊登

d) 替報紙訂閱打廣告

題解：文章第一句即表明此訊息目的在招募人才，主要負責訂閱業務（sell subscriptions），故答案選 b) 最適當。

2. 解答：b) 年滿十八歲

中譯：

唯一的應徵條件是什麼？

a) 有開朗的個性

b) 年滿十八歲

c) 能夠挨家挨戶拜訪

d) 工作勤奮努力

題解：由文章倒數第二句關鍵句 "You could be that person if you are over the age of 18." 可知，這項工作的要求是必需年滿十八歲，故答案選 b)。

25

Cover Letter
求職信

25

閱讀重點 ......

求職信（cover letter）用來回應公司的徵才廣告，主要內容包括申請者
（applicant）想應徵的工作職位，並簡述自己的學經歷。本文以應徵電腦產業
的求職信為例，其閱讀重點如下：

① 寫信目的：回應 Ms. Frago 在 Los Angeles Times 的徵才廣告。
② 個人特質及優勢：電腦產業的豐富經驗、畢業於加州大學洛杉機分校。

文章閱讀 ......

Cover Letter

STEPHANIE HAUGEN
1218 Dunwich Avenue, Torrance, CA 90502

Telephone/Fax: (310) 320-9224

e-mail: shaugen@ubu.com

February 2, 2001

Dear Ms. Frago,

I am writing to you **in reference to** the ad you have placed in the January 30th edition of the *Los Angeles Times*.

As you will note in the **enclosed** resume, I have had extensive experience in the field of computers. Since my graduation from UCLA, I have had the chance to work with top firms in the computer industry. I feel that <u>with my knowledge and expertise,</u> I can be an asset to your organization. I hope that you will give me the opportunity to show this.

Please feel free to **contact** me at any time. I **look forward to** hearing from you.

Sincerely yours,

Stephanie Haugen

● 學習焦點 ●●●

應徵工作的信件通常都有以下的重點：

① 個人資訊：包括姓名（STEPHANIE HAUGEN）、地址、電話、email 信箱等。

② 第一段表明寫信目的："I am writing to you in reference to the ad you have placed in the January 30th edition of the *Los Angeles Times*." 表示本文是回應 Ms. Frago 於一月三十日在《洛杉磯時報》刊登的徵人廣告。

③ 第二段主要是敘述自己的優勢，引起收信人 Ms. Frago 的注目，參考附件中的履歷（the enclosed resume），包括自己的學歷及經歷 "Since my graduation from UCLA, I have had the chance to work with top firms in the computer industry." （從加州大學洛杉磯分校畢業後，我有幸在電腦業界幾家頂尖公司工作過。）

④ 接著再順勢預期自己如果獲得任用，將會對該公司有所貢獻 "I feel that with my knowledge and expertise, I can be an asset to your organization." ；並希望對方給自己這個機會證明所言非虛 "I hope that you will give me the opportunity to show this." 。

⑤ 最後則以期待對方的回應做結語：" I look forward to hearing from you." 。

🌐 語言知識補充站 ··

⭐ **Vocabulary**

＊ in reference to：關於
用法：in reference to ＋ 參考的事物 / 資料
I am writing to you / in reference to the ad / you have placed / in the January 30th edition of the *Los Angeles Times*.
我寫信給你 / 關於一個廣告 / 你曾刊登 / 在一月三十日的《洛杉磯時報》

＊ enclose：【動詞】夾帶；附帶
As you will note / in the enclosed resume, / I have had extensive experience / in the field of computers.
正如你將會注意 / 在這份隨函附上的履歷裡 / 我有豐富經驗 / 在電腦領域

＊ contact：【動詞】與……接觸
Please feel free to / contact me / at any time.
請隨意 / 與我聯絡 / 在任何時間

＊ look forward to：期待；盼望
用法：look forward to ＋ V-ing / 期盼的事物

I / look forward to / hearing from you.
我 / 期待 / 聽到你的消息。

＊求職信（cover letter）中常見的字彙：
experience（經驗）、knowledge（知識）、 expertise（專業技能）、asset（資產；特質）。

★ Sentence Pattern

以片語開頭的句型：（Phrase）, S + V

本句型通常有因果關係或附帶狀況，也就是在片語所描述的前提下，對後面主要的句子有何影響。

With my knowledge and expertise, I can be an asset to your organization.
　　　　　　　　　　　　　↑

表示「在我所具備的知識及專業技能的前提下」，所以會有後面 "I can be an asset to your organization."（我會成為貴單位的資產。）

📖 摘要與測驗重點提示 ••

★ 閱讀要項

求職信屬於應用文體，都是以直接、明確的文字說明以下必要資訊：

① 寫信目的：in reference to the ad you have placed in the January 30th
　　　　　　 edition of the *Los Angeles Times*
② 個人學歷：graduation from UCLA
③ 特殊經歷：extensive experience in the field of computers, working with top
　　　　　　 firms in the computer industry

★ 常用字彙及句法

① 表明寫信的依據：in reference to ＋ 參考的事物 / 資料
② 常用於信件的結語：look forward to ＋ V-ing / 期盼的事物

★ 測驗重點

本文章的主要目的是吸引收信人的興趣，對求職者印象深刻，得到面談機會。

練習題

1. What kind of document is this?

a) A resume

b) A cover letter

c) A letter to the editor of a publication

d) A letter of recommendation

2. Why was this letter written?

a) To apply for a job

b) To reply to a letter from Ms. Fargo

c) To sell computer software

d) To keep in touch

Cover Letter

Dear Mr. Patterson,

Enclosed is the résumé you requested detailing my experience in marketing and advertising. As you will see, I have worked in many fields, including real estate, consumer electronics, and the Internet.

I feel I can make a contribution to your company because of my experience and also because of our shared philosophy of marketing that we discussed over the phone.

I will contact you next week and hopefully we can meet to discuss specifically how I can assist you and your company in expanding your market share.

If you have any questions, please feel free to call me anytime.

Sincerely,

Ron Brown

1. Which sentence is NOT true?

a) The letter writer will call Mr. Patterson.

b) He wants to help the company grow.

c) He would like a job in marketing.

d) He has not spoken with Mr. Patterson yet.

2. What kind of letter is this?

a) A cover letter

b) A letter of complaint

c) A letter of introduction

d) A chain letter

3. Who is Mr. Brown?

a) A former employee

b) A prospective employee

c) A friend of Mr. Patterson

d) Mr. Patterson's marketing managers

文章閱讀 翻譯與題解

● 文章翻譯 ‧‧

求職信

STEPHANIE HAUGEN

1218 Dunwich Avenue, Torrance, CA 90502

電話 / 傳真：(310) 320-9224

電子郵件信箱：shaugen@ubu.com

2012 年 2 月 2 日

親愛的 Fargo 女士，

寫這封信是回應您在 1 月 30 日《洛杉磯時報》上所刊登的廣告。

隨信附上個人簡歷，敝人具備豐富的電腦相關經歷。從美國加州大學洛杉磯分校畢業後，即獲得在頂尖電腦公司工作的機會。相信本人的知識和技術必能為貴公司帶來貢獻。希望您能給我機會證明這一點。

歡迎隨時與我聯絡。期盼您的回信。

Stephanie Haugen 敬上

題解 ••

1. 解答：b) 求職信

中譯：

這是什麼類型的文件？

a) 履歷

b) 求職信

c) 給出版社主編的信

d) 推薦函

題解：由開頭表明求職目的，以及第二段簡述個人經歷可判斷，這是一封求職信（cover letter），故答案選 b)。

2. 解答：a) 為了應徵工作

中譯：

為什麼要寫這封信？

a) 為了應徵工作

b) 為了回覆 Fargo 女士的信

c) 為了推銷電腦軟體

d) 為了保持聯絡

題解：由信中開頭第一句可知，作者因為看到報紙的徵才廣告，所以寫了這封求職信，故答案選 a)。apply for「應徵；申請（工作、職位）」。

● 文章翻譯 ••

求職信

親愛的 Patterson 先生，

　　附上的履歷是依照您的要求詳述個人在廣告和行銷方面之經驗。如您所見，我曾在許多領域工作過，包含房地產業、消費性電子產品業和網路業。

　　相信憑藉個人的經驗，以及我們在電話中所談到的共通行銷理念，我必能為貴公司帶來貢獻。

　　我將於下週與您聯絡，希望我們可以見面討論，尤其談談如何協助您和貴公司擴大市佔率。

　　如果您有任何疑問，歡迎隨時與我聯絡。

Ron Brown 敬上

● 題解 ••

1. 解答：d) 他未曾和 Patterson 先生交談過。

中譯：

下列哪個描述為非？

a) 寫這封信的人會打電話給 Patterson 先生。

b) 他希望協助這間公司成長茁壯。

c) 他希望獲得行銷方面的職務。

d) 他未曾和 Patterson 先生交談過。

題解： 由文章第二段提到的 "…we discussed over the phone." 可推知，寄信者 Ron 曾和 Patterson 先生通過電話，故答案 d) 的描述不正確。

2. 解答：a) 求職信

中譯：

這是什麼類型的信件？

a) 求職信

b) 抱怨信

c) 介紹信

d) 連鎖信

題解： 由文章中的關鍵字詞 résumé（履歷）、簡述自身工作經驗並要求進一步面談的內容，可看出這是封求職信，故選 a)。

3. 解答：b) 可能被雇用的員工

中譯：

Brown 先生是誰？

a) 離職員工

b) 可能被雇用的員工

c) Patterson 先生的朋友

d) Patterson 先生的行銷主管

題解： 由寄信者的署名可知，Brown 先生寫信的目的是應徵工作，由此判斷他是可能被雇用的員工，故答案選 b)。prospective 是形容詞「預期的；可能的」。

Global English
全球英語閱讀力

2012年8月初版　　　　　　　　　　　　　　　　　　定價：新臺幣380元
有著作權‧翻印必究
Printed in Taiwan.

主　　　編	陳　超　明
編　　　著	TOEIC 900 工作團隊
發　行　人	林　載　爵

出　版　者	聯經出版事業股份有限公司	叢書編輯	李　　　芃
地　　　址	台北市基隆路一段180號4樓	資料整理	李　靜　儀
編輯部地址	台北市基隆路一段180號4樓		呂　虹　瑾
叢書主編電話	(02)87876242轉226	整體設計	江　宜　蔚
台北聯經書房	台北市新生南路三段94號	錄音後製	純粹錄音後製公司
電　　　話	(02)23620308		
台中分公司	台中市北區健行路321號1樓		
暨門市電話	(04)22371234ext.5		
郵政劃撥帳戶	第0100559-3號		
郵撥電話	(02)23620308		
印　刷　者	文聯彩色製版印刷有限公司		
總　經　銷	聯合發行股份有限公司		
發　行　所	台北縣新店市寶橋路235巷6弄6號2樓		
電　　　話	(02)29178022		

行政院新聞局出版事業登記證局版臺業字第0130號

本書如有缺頁，破損，倒裝請寄回台北聯經書房更換。　　ISBN　978-957-08-4035-3 (平裝)
聯經網址：www.linkingbooks.com.tw
電子信箱：linking@udngroup.com

國家圖書館出版品預行編目資料

全球英語閱讀力/陳超明主編 . TOEIC 900
工作團隊編著 . 初版 . 臺北市 . 聯經 . 2012年8月
（民101年）. 304面 . 17×23公分（Global English）
ISBN 978-957-08-4035-3（平裝附光碟）

1.英語 2.讀本

805.18   101013870